THE ACADEMY

Reagan Kaiser

For Jaci

Thank you for always being there for me, and being my biggest fan.
Thank you for loving this story even when I wasn't sure of it.

For my friends

Thank you for being just that, my friends. It truly means the world to
me to have you here with me, especially now that I've reached out
and achieved my dreams.

There are so many people whom this book is based on, and I hope
each one realizes that it is them as they read. Thank you all, sorry
for people-watching you guys while writing ;)

Chapter 1

Ah, damn. Today is orientation day.

That's good news and bad news. The good news is that the demons will be easy tonight-the bad news is that a whole new group of freshman will need to deal with this place for the next four years. I slink back to my classroom's dorm. It's been empty since the seniors have graduated. I'm a junior, so to speak. I've been here three years.

There are no windows in this place, no way out but to graduate or to die. We weren't sent to this place because we're bad people. As a matter of fact we were sent here because we're too good, delicate, and fragile. I almost feel bad for the poor freshman. All I'm going to hear tonight is screaming and fear and disbelief- a third of the freshman class will die tonight.

I smirk, remembering my freshman orientation day. *I didn't want to come here, the seniors all claimed that people die here. But here I was, my parents so proud of me. They thought that I wanted to come here. No. I was too scared to come here. But I stood outside the gates, looking onto the creepy old building. There were absolutely no windows that I could see, all of them were boarded up. Was that even allowed?*

A man came out hunched over his cane. He was very pale and sickly looking with deep gray eyes and a forbidding stare. His very fine, light gray hair hardly moved in the breeze. His voice shocked me. It was deep and rough and strong. "Hello students, parents. Welcome to the Academy. As you should know, your child was sent an invitation to join this school. That is an honor. They will have no classes, no homework. They will live in dorm rooms with their class mates, male and female. There is perfect equality; you are all seen as students." He paused for a moment, then began to address us students specifically, telling us what we were to expect when he continued." You will be trained for the outside world and the dangers that lie within. This school is neither for the faint of heart, nor those who believe that any God can and will save them. Here, you are on your own. This is my warning. You may either leave with your student, or say goodbye to them. You will not see them or hear from them in the next four years."

About half the crowd looked uneasy, the other half looked excited. Not one person left though. We would come to find later that it was a mistake, a terrible mistake. I said goodbye to my parents and my little brother. "Do not let him come here." I begged them. "Please, I have a very bad feeling about this."

"If he's invited, we'll think about it. By the time he's ready for high school, you'll be out and able to tell us. C'mon, it can't be so bad." They relentlessly pushed me. I rolled my eyes and hugged each of them, my heart pounding. Then we were lead away.

Once we got inside the building, the door sealed tight behind us. "I hope you know how to swim." The headmaster said. "At this school, you will be fighting demons at every turn. Many of you will die and will never again see your parents. I would suggest you keep on edge and expect the worst. And if you don't know how to swim, you'd better learn by nightfall." We didn't ever see the headmaster after that. We got to our dorm rooms and we were completely shocked. Along the walls were weapons, survival packs, and all sorts of things. I found flotation devices, and put them in my pillow. I knew how to swim but I wasn't taking any chances. A nervous looking boy, whose bed was across from mine, did the same.

I went over to him, "Can't swim?"

"Oh no, I can. I can swim like a fish. I just want to be on the safe side, you know?" He replied.

"Same. My name is Reagan, by the way." I told him.

"I'm Jaci, nice to meet you. Let's get through these four years, alright?" He said.

I smiled, "Yeah. Now let's get a pack." We headed to the wall and grabbed the pack with our names on them. Inside there was a fold up scythe, a box of BBs, dried packs of food in waterproof containers, a waterproof box filled with lighters and matches, a hatchet, a small machete, and a very strong belt. I put the belt on and put the hatchet in its sheath on the belt, and slid the machete on the strap that went across my back. There was also a sewing kit, and other helpful necessities. I put the scythe in my now floatable pillow. I took a sheet of fireproof material and quickly stitched it to my blanket.

Jaci came over to me, "Would you please do that for mine? He said demons, and if there is a dragon I would love a shield you know?" I smile and stitch on the material to his blanket. That was how I made my first friend at the Academy.

Now these freshmen have to deal with it. My first night, about 100 people drowned. When one grade gets punished or tested, all the other grades suffer with them. Regular demons and ghosts come nightly; some attacks are during the day. Jaci has actually become more than friends with me. We started dating during our second year, and we teamed up to take down monsters together. We train with each other and we are the reason we're both still alive. Alliances are helpful, too.

Soon, shaky little freshman start coming in. We got 13 freshmen. Great. I am on my bed, sharpening my blades. Jaci and I are the only juniors. There are 12 sophomores. No seniors. Jaci and I are both 16. Instead of driving, we're throwing knives. Instead of parties, we're hunting monsters. Instead of life, we're training. Jaci is nine months older than me. We made a deal, when he graduates he's taking me with him. In return I watch his back, keep him safe.

"So." Jaci calls to the freshman. "What was today's warning?"

"Hope you like fire and fairy tales because I have a real treat for you tonight." Quoted a freshman girl. She looks at Jaci with some sort of awe.

I look over at him. "Hey Jaci, let's build a castle."

He smiles, he knows what I mean. "Already built. We built it years ago. Never thought he'd actually throw a dragon our way. Want to get a tan and cuddle?"

"Sounds good to me." I say. "Freshmen and sophomores, the wood of your bed is fire proof, it will never catch fire. I'd suggest you find the fire protective material, and use it." I drag my blanket off my bed. "This is what it looks like, you can stitch it on your own blankets and just hide under the covers during the attack. Don't get used to that. Sleep tight, and don't forget to get your packs. You have about an hour until curfew. Go."

I grab my pack. The material is completely life proof, fire proof and water tight. You could shoot a bullet and it wouldn't harm the bag or the contents. It's completely indestructible, and the size of a large backpack. It's been a very helpful shield. I stand on Jaci's bed and pull down the fireproof/water resistant curtain we've made.

I've kind of always wanted a dragon to attack. Since when was a dragon supposed to be easy? I guess I would have to see. I crawl under the fort of blankets and one of the new freshman boys called "Are you two going to do the dirty?!"

"Oh shut up." Jaci giggled.

"Guys c'mon he can't be serious. You can't expect me to believe that a dragon is going to come and destroy our lives." The boy complains.

"Then have fun dying!" I call and curl up to Jaci. The freshman snorts in disbelief. Idiot. He's really going to get himself killed. "Think of it this way, better safe than sorry right?"

He grumbles to himself and I can't see what he's doing. I peek out and there are 5 more canopies like the one Jaci and I built. The sophomores saw the idea and liked it. Good, it should keep them safe.

I can hear the hustle and bustle of freshman hurrying around. I'm almost excited for their orientation. It just means that they need to start believing that they've been welcomed into Hell. Why would parents just allow their children to be taken away and locked up for four years? I wonder from time to time if my parents remember me. Or my little brother. I wonder if they miss me.

These kinds of thoughts come around every year on orientation day. This is the only day I allow my focus to be deterred from survival.

The time is ticking away and darkness is slowly setting in. The freshmen in the room light the lamps, silly freshmen. The dragon is going to come and blow fire anyway. It's such a waste of lighter fluid and matches.

Jaci wraps his arms around me and kisses my head. In the midst of the Academy trying to show us that the world is evil, I have found my corner of light. I am going to cling to it for my life. The class that I'm in, which is consisted of the people with whom I share a dorm, is close knit. There are a few more couples like Jaci and I. Samie, my friend, is dating a boy named Jared. They're sophomores. Samie is 17; I don't know how she's a grade under me, or dating a 15 year old. I haven't got the heart to tell her she can't bring Jared with her when she graduates because he's too young.

One of the freshmen, a female, calls out "Its night time. Why hasn't the dragon come yet? Were you just pulling our legs?"

Oh! The dragon hasn't come yet! I take our canopy and secure it under the mattress. Our weight should hold it down so it can't flutter in the breeze of the ferocious fire. We are totally encased in a dark box of fire protection. "It'll come when you least expect it." I reply. I lean forward and kiss Jaci gently on the lips, never know when it's going to be our last kiss.

It's silent in the room, everyone is in bed. Many of kids partnered up. It's hard to be alone through the night, especially here. I can just hardly hear breathing. Minutes pass before the telltale *creaaaaak!* on the stairs. The attack has just begun. I hold tightly to Jaci. I'm nervous, I'm always nervous. People will die tonight and there is always a possibility that I, or someone I love, will be numbered among the dead.

Then came the first scream. Shortly following came "*IT'S A FREAKING DRAGON!*"

Oh this was going to be good. I curl up to Jaci, holding him tight just to feel the comfort of his embrace as things begin to light up. The room gets bright, really bright. People are screaming. The light flickers in shades of gold and orange. The heat is incredible; it has to be no less than 120 degrees Fahrenheit in our canopy box. I can't even imagine how hot it is in the fire.

I know with no doubt that it's really a dragon when this creature lets out a ferocious roar. This roar shakes me to the bones, terrifying me. I grip my scythe. Its curved blade has protected me against scaly demons numerous times before. Jaci and I both sit up, each gripping blades to protect us in case the dragon uses its claws. This was going on in every dorm for every class through the whole castle. Tonight, each dragon will pick one student as its dinner. I'm hoping its one of the crispy students, the precooked ones.

A piercing scream comes from one of the freshman girls and a resounding roar from the dragon follows shortly after. It looks like the dragon has caught its late night snack. Jaci and I wait for about 10 minutes to exit our box canopy.

"That was much easier than expected. Normally you have to fight. So, do you believe us now?" Jaci snaps at the 6 remaining freshman. "You have to stay on guard, always."

"What if it comes back?" Sobs a girl, the very one who had taken an interest in Jaci. She hugs him and I look at her with my eye brow raised. Some just want to be murdered.

"You're safe for the night." Jaci replies stiffly, trying to lean back from the clingy girl. "Go to bed, all of you. Believe me you'll want your sleep. We'll wake you when it's time for breakfast." He pries the girl off him. "What's your name?"

"I'm Emma."

"Okay Emma. Go to bed, please." I say coldly. She shoots me an icy glare, and lets go of Jaci. I go and kiss him on the cheek. Everyone crawls into bed, some alone and some with someone special. Of course my train of thought has been sparked. Is this Emma chick going to try to steal Jaci from me? It is allowed for the students to teach others a lesson.

I wonder how many freshmen have died tonight. We would have to hold a count in the morning. We should also probably think of a name for our class, so the freshmen know where to return to.

Why did this school ever come to be? Who had the idea to torture children until there was nothing but fear and hate left? What was the goal in that? Was there an ulterior motive? I hate it but, I can't help but wonder these things each night, keeping me from the sleep that I need. Not like it was good sleep. I always hate when the freshmen roll through, it reminds me that this awful place was real and eating more innocence. God knows it's taken mine.

I hold Jaci close and close my eyes, falling into another restless sleep. I knew that I wouldn't dream tonight but I guess sometimes that's what I wish.

Chapter 2

It's tough to make friends in a new setting. Now, try making friends when today could be your last day. If that doesn't make you paranoid, you're lying to yourself. It's impossible to be truly happy when you are paranoid all the time. I'll admit it. I'm scared. Anything could happen, you know? I'm so afraid of that. I've become a hard, cold person through this whole ordeal, don't get me wrong, but it is possible that I could die any day.

I just want to know...why? Why on earth would someone open the Academy? It's cruel-what do they tell the parents of the dead? "We're sorry; a dragon ate your child. But here- you can have the ashes of their charred skin before taking them away for a slow, painful death"? Why hasn't someone tried to shut this place down?

I groan as I start waking up. I hated being semi conscious just before waking up, it almost guarantees thought. Lord knows we can't have *that*.

I shake Jaci awake. "C'mon sleepy head, time to get up." He opens his eyes, instantly awake and distrusting. It actually hurts that he doesn't trust being woken up. He simply doesn't trust much. It took me forever to earn his trust.

We crawl out from under the sheets and walk into the common area. Three people are gathered there. "Ah. Go getters." I say sarcastically.

They're all freshman. "We don't want to die." One says. The other two nod. That's great, a clique.

"I am telling you right now that is the worst attitude to have. You have to NOT be afraid to die. Then you can attack and defend more freely, giving you an even higher survival rate. You'd unlock your shell and break free." I reply. "That's a helpful tip. Go wake the others."

They scamper off and I grab my uniform off the wall. It's like a soldier's, almost. I wear tight black pants, made of heavy leather to protect my skin. The shirt is a mottled gray, and fitted. I tie up my wavy brown hair into a tight bun, to keep it out of the way. It's how I dress every day. The bun is a personal choice but it has definitely proved helpful.

Slowly, all the rest of my class piles into the common area. The six freshmen are rubbing their eyes. The sophomores are already awake and alert, rushing to put on their uniforms.

"Alright then, freshmen." I call out to them. "We have half an hour until breakfast, and we're safe until after breakfast. I'm Reagan, and this is Jaci." I gesture to where Jaci is strapping on his weapons. "We're the only two juniors, and the oldest. The seniors are either dead or home. We'll be the ones helping you out. Now, whatever you think isn't real, it is. Get rid of any disbelieve here. There are monsters, demons, ghosts. There is evil. And it will kill you. I've watched friends die, ripped to pieces.

"What I'm wearing right now is school uniform. Ladies- either cut your hair to the length of boys or tie it up in a bun. This way it doesn't get caught on something." Jaci pipes in. "Always carry your pack and weapons on you. You will be caught off guard. Every summer, we get exactly one month worry free. Yesterday, your orientation day, marks the day that the monsters return. We call it summer break."

I let him finish then I continue. "You can have friendships and relationships within the group and school, but if you cause drama the students can 'punish' other students. If you try to unlawfully punish another student, say they didn't do anything wrong, you are fed to the vampires. Vampires don't just drink from your neck-they tear you to shreds."

I notice Emma flinch, maybe now she'll leave Jaci alone. "Get dressed, breakfast is soon. You really don't want to miss an important meal. Remember, classrooms get punished if one student does something that breaks the rules, like look outside. It could be poison in their food, or a haunt that attacks daily. So be good. We don't have something that attacks us daily yet. Don't break anything at breakfast. The headmaster doesn't like that. Don't make a mess in the halls. Make sure you make your bed. And if you go swimming, be careful of what's in the water."

The freshmen are hurrying to get changed. "Do you have a hair tie?" Emma asks me.

"Nope, use a leather strap. It's stronger anyway." I hint her.

"Let's hurry; I want to get back to the dorm BEFORE something attacks." Jared calls. Samie nods in agreement. The sophomores are out the door, a few of the freshman following them. I'm left with Jaci and Emma.

I take Jaci's hand. "Let's go."

"So... Why is this school here?" Emma decides to chatter as we're walking towards the dining hall.

"To teach the good people that there is bad in the world, and to teach them fear." I reply.

"Oh... So why don't we have a haunt yet?" She asks again.

"We're a good group of students. The better you are, the less attacks you suffer. I should also mention; no drugs or alcohol. That'll get you killed." Jaci said.

"What happens if someone does get drugs or alcohol?"

"Then we're going to be slaughtered, picked off one by one, by a haunt." I snarl. Emma goes pale, and we walk in silence until we reach the dining hall, or cafe.

I have to admit, this school is pretty. The Academy was built to be a millionaire private school, but became what it is today. The dining hall has very high, pointed ceilings with wooden rafters. The floor is granite tile, and the tables are huge circular tables that could fit entire classes. They're made of glossy cherry birch wood. There are candle-lit chandeliers every 10 feet, which shine quite brightly against the granite. It's a very pretty room.

"Someone could get married in here!" Emma gasps.

"You won't think that for long. C'mon, to our classroom's table." I reply.

"So why are they called classrooms?" She asks.

I'm getting really tired of her questions, but I did say if they had any questions... "We're called classrooms because it is a school. We're actually teams. We work together and look out for each other. We respect each other."

When we sit, the familiar little troll runs to our table and serves us plates of food. The food is always hot and good, and I've never been poisoned. "Thanks Pedro!" I call to the troll as he stumbles away. He growls in return, I wonder if he likes that name.

Breakfast today is sausage, eggs, a muffin, and bacon. It is delicious. I'm eating merrily and talking to Jaci when I see a male freshman in our classroom grab his throat, his eyes bulging. He's not choking; he would be turning purple instead of green. Someone leaps up and rushes over to him and I catch them before they go any further- "Stop." I say. "It's useless. He's been poisoned." I continue eating.

"Why?!" The person who leapt up to help him asks.

"He must have brought drugs or alcohol to breakfast. The headmaster knows everything, and that is the only reason he would be poisoned." I answer. "The antidote is in one of your other foods; you just have to find it quickly."

The guy who leapt up to help him is shoveling food down his throat, but the boy goes limp before all of the food has been fitted in. He's dead.

Pedro the troll comes back out and carries away the boy's body, and everyone is too shocked to do anything. I say, "Keep eating. You don't get to eat in peace again until dinner."

"You call this peace?!" One of the girls starts to cry.

"Yep." Samie says. "The rules are simple, just don't break them."

The freshmen, now 5 in number, start eating slowly. They're unsettled. It's funny, they don't want to believe. They thought this was a prank. I can see it in their eyes, they believe it now. They now know that they have to tough up and obey the rules. That's how you'll survive this game. That is exactly what it is. It's a game.

"Hurry, we've got to get back to the dorm." Jared says. "Our attack is about to begin." The ceiling overhead shakes and dust rains down on us, proving Jared's point. We all quickly stand and start dashing to our dorm room.

We get there in almost record time and Jaci starts shouting orders. "Wield your weapons-we don't know what we're fighting yet. Get into your best defensive stance. Use your back pack as a shield; it's built to be indestructible. Quick! It's coming!"

I stand beside Jaci and we take a defensive stance together, he has his machete in his hand and I extend my scythe to the length of a reaper's. Mine is the only one that does that, I modified it. The school actually encourages craftiness in the form of modifying and creating new weapons, I made a powerful long bow and BB tipped arrows. It does some incredible damage. I lay the longbow at my feet with a quiver of my arrows. I took a whole summer break to do that.

I look around, the freshmen are scared. It's okay to be scared. "Freshmen, wear your backpacks on the front of your torso so you can use both hands. Whatever this thing is, it won't care if you're new. It will kill you."

Quickly, they listen to me. Their torsos are covered completely, like armor. Within moments, our common area door bangs open against the wall, splintering the wood. A monster runs in hissing. It is really tall, nearly skimming the high ceilings. It is completely black and incredibly thin-it looks like we could snap it in half. The skin, however, is jagged and looks hard and leathery. Its eyes are also black, but shining like beetles. It opens its mouth horrifyingly wide, and you can see rows of jagged and gray teeth. It roars loudly, saliva spraying from its mouth. I don't know what the heck this thing is. I've never seen it before. When it extends spiked wings, someone gasps quietly, "Jabberwocky."

Isn't the Jabberwocky a creature that was written about in a poem somewhere? Where did the headmaster get one of these babes? "Take off the head, if it's a Jabberwocky then that's the only way to kill it." I yell. The Jabberwocky turns its head to me, and I jump when these fin like things snap off from behind his head, making him look two times bigger.

That's right, Reagan. I can hear in in my head. *You've got to kill me to live, don't you?* I am completely frozen and it starts stalking over to me. *Well, human, it's kill or be killed.* I sink to my knees, helpless. I can't move, can't lift my arms, can't stop it. Why can't I?

Why can't I? It hisses and raises it's claws, about to sweep down on me and tear me to shreds. I break my trance quickly and look around, everyone else is frozen. I leap up and scream, "COME AT ME!"

The Jabberwocky looks confused, wondering how I managed to break my spell. I run at him with my Scythe fully extended. The Jabberwocky roars and I smile, delighted to be taking on a haunt by myself. I run straight at it and just as it swings its claws down, I duck and roll to the side. It turns its head to me and I swing my scythe, taking out the eyes. It roars in pain and anger, no longer able to see me. I am still the greater foe, so he ignores the helpless people on the floor. I stalk silently all the way around it to the other side and lift my scythe above his neck. I walk under his neck and retract my scythe, cutting off the head in the process. The head falls with a *thump* right behind me. The blood splatters the wall and the floor and the people who are no longer motionless, and drips down onto me.

Jaci rushes up to me and hugs me. "That was incredibly risky!" He scolds me.

"If I hadn't done it you all would have died, and then our whole classroom would have been wiped out." I reply.

Jaci sighs and kisses my cheek. "Well done, though. Very well done."

"Was that our haunt of the day?" Emma asks me, a spark of fear and respect in her eyes. I smirk, now I know she'll respect my relationship.

"For the day time, yes. I'm glad that was over quickly, we have the rest of the daytime hours free to ourselves. I'd suggest training or preparing for anything. It's a totally dangerous place here. I don't think you want to be caught off guard." I reply. "Get familiar with your surrounding in this room. Know where everything is, what everything is. Stay out of trouble or else we'll be in for a whole lot more."

Jaci turns to me. "Want to go train?"

"Yeah, let's go." I say. I take his hand and we walk out. We walk down the familiar halls. We're not immune to any creatures, so I have my scythe fully extended in one hand, and Jaci has his hatchet. "What are we going to work on today?"

"I'm thinking upper-body strength, both triceps and biceps. Then we can work on cardio and leg strength. Finish it off with some core. Then, after the strength training, does hand-to-hand combat sound good?"

"Yeah, sounds like a full work out." I answer. We get into the large gym. In one half, there are mats for sparring. There are a few kids there, tumbling about. In the other half is a full-blown gym, filled with work out equipment that looks like it cost thousands of dollars. Jaci and I walk to the side with the equipment and set our bags at our feet. We each have a lock on the pack so no one can steal from us, and the keys are around our necks. Stealing was encouraged here, but punished if you were caught. I've never been caught but I've stolen enough to build three packs. I shared the loot with Jaci and Samie. I was interested in the BBs; I don't know why we had them if firearms weren't allowed on the premises.

Anyways, Jaci and I look around. It looks like there isn't anyone on the equipment but us. "So who's going first?" I ask. We take turns so we can keep an eye out for trouble, as well as help each other train.

"You go first; you've earned it with the slaying of the Jabberwocky." Jaci answers.

We like to work out; it stretches our muscles and gives us hope. It gives us the hope that we'll be strong enough to graduate. It gives us a purpose and a way to pass time and it makes us strong and fit and survival ready. I don't want to be one of those people who, when the time comes, is too weak to complete the task at hand.

Chapter 3

So I get to train first. It's nice, it really is. I look over to Jaci and just before I can start working out, the floor shakes. Just great. "Looks like we've got an attack coming." I state.

It's obvious that the other students in the gym notice it, too. I quickly unlock my pack and pull out my machete and strap it across my back, and sheathe the hatchet on my hip. I extend my scythe and wield it, ready to take action. Jaci is wielding his machete; it's not hard to tell that it's his favorite weapon.

The other students take their defensive stance, and I look back to Jaci. Whatever it is, it sounds mean. Jaci and I wear our backpacks on our torsos. I had stitched the fireproof material to them in freshman year, they were completely indestructible.

Jaci nearly laughs. "This will have to serve as training." He glances at me. "You ready love?"

"Yes I am." I say. "Are you?" It's a lie.

He nods curtly. No one is ever ready for this. There is no door to the gym, just a wide open archway. We all pose, facing the archway, because it's the only entrance in the school. The floor shakes again, and this time we hear a screeching with it. It's an unnatural shriek, inhuman. From my bag I pulled out two pairs of earplugs, and hand one to Jaci. Very quickly we shoved them in our ears and grab our weapons, getting into the stance again. I feel like the haunt is a Banshee of some sort. Better safe than sorry.

Then comes another shriek, it's barely audible through the plugs. This is incredible, because these earplugs can block out up to 250dB of noise. That's the amount of sound from standing next to a canon as it shoots, louder than a firearm. 250dB is enough to cause you to go deaf if heard for more than 5 minutes straight per day. I would love to know the strength of the noise. It has to be a banshee. Well, I guess I was always prepared. It's good to have a backup plan. I had battled a banshee once before- the only way to destroy it is by fire.

A banshee is an angry spirit, always female, who died violently. They are ghostly, and are generally hovering about a foot off the ground. They are incredibly scary looking. Their piercing shrieks can rupture your eardrums until you're on your knees, clutching your bloody ears. The second shriek would pop all the blood vessels in your face, neck, and eyes. The third- your eyes would explode. It's a vicious way to die. With the earplugs, the worst she can do to me and Jaci is put a ringing in our ears for days and dizzy us.

Banshees can't kill in any way except screeching. They can't physically touch a person. If you piss one off, its shriek can shatter ground. It's a ground breaking achievement, if I do say so. The chandeliers overhead swing, the lights flicker. She's about to enter the room.

"Kill it with fire!" I yell out. I can't hear myself at all. The other students turn to me and nod. The Banshee enters the room and is silent.

She is about 7 feet tall and a foot and a half above the ground. Her hair is straggly, going down her back and hanging in front of her face. She is limp, face towards the floor. She is wearing a white nightgown that is ripped and stained. I grab my bow and light an arrow on fire, and launch it at her. She looks up, revealing black, soul-less eyes and shrieks. She catches the arrow in mid air and blows out the flame, the arrow sailing through her harmlessly. She shrieks again, at the other students. I see their faces contort in pain as they shrink to their knees. I run over towards her, Jaci close behind. I light another arrow and aim it at her. She seems to smirk as she watches me. Jaci sneaks up behind her with his match and lights it. I smile as he sets her nightgown aflame. She doesn't notice until it's too late.

Soon, the banshee is engulfed in flames. It's a lot like setting fire to paper. Her skin curls up and blackens. She shrieks as she burns, but in pain rather than spite. It's almost like she is suffering. It's actually kind of painful to listen to. I even feel *sorry* for her.

That banshee burns, but instead of completely disappearing, one claw falls from her. It lies on the ground, black smoke emitting from it. It's a spoil of war, and it belongs to Jaci now. Spoils of war are the remains of something that someone has killed. They bring incredibly good luck. Jaci grabs it and puts it in his pocket. I make a mental note to make a necklace from it for him later. Jaci and I head over to the other students and extend our hands, helping them up. I take out my earplugs and the noise is startling.

"Th-thank you!" gasps one student. "We would have died back there. You really are prepared for everything, aren't you?" he asks.

"Yeah. You guys are what, sophomores?" I answer.

"Yeah. You must be a junior." The boy winks at me. "You may be the elder student but I'm sure I could teach you a thing or two." He proceeds to walk closer.

Jaci strides up to him. "Back off." He snarls.

The sophomore looks scared. "Y-yeah, sorry man. I didn't know she was taken." They slink away.

I turn and kiss Jaci. "That was pretty awesome, man. Good job. I've never seen a banshee do that though."

"I haven't either. I don't think it was for us." With that, Jaci turns his gaze to the sophomores, who were standing in the entrance. "Oi! What did you do to get a banshee on your backs?"

"It's our daily haunt." They mope.

"Then why the heck don't you have ear plugs! Go get some! Or else next time you'll be dead because my girlfriend and I won't be there to save your sorry butts!" Jaci yells. They run off, hopefully to get earplugs. Idiots.

"Well at least it was a halfway decent work out!" I laugh.

Jaci's not in a good mood, the idiocy of others pisses him off. "All we did was teamwork! Which is good, but boring as anything." I roll my eyes at him, he's such a guy. "Let's get back to the dorm before they think we've snuck off somewhere." he finishes.

"It wouldn't be the first time," I say under my breath. He must have heard me because he rolls his eyes and slaps my butt. I yelp and we giggle as we walk back to the dorm. We aren't holding hands, because we're still on guard from the attack.

When we get back, Emma asks us, "How was training?"

Jaci replies, sullen, "We didn't get to do much training. We had to help some sophomores fight a banshee."

"Why didn't you just run?" The snarky freshman boy asks. I wonder what his name is, and how hard it would be to crack his thick skull.

"If you run, you die. I don't know how but I've seen it- the cowards just drop dead." Samie butts in.

"Well that's absolutely great" Laughs that snarky freshman.

"What is your name?" I snap.

"Aaron." He winks at me and nods, saying, "You can call me master though, babe."

I walk up to him and slap him clean across the face. It has a loud snapping noise, and he looks at me with hate and awe. There is a large red hand print across his face. "You need to learn to respect your freaking elders as they're the ones who are going to save your behind time and time again, got it? We all need to cooperate and even be friends if you want to make it to graduation! Right now you're on the wrong track because Jaci would snap your neck without hesitation for hitting on me. Calm yourself down and focus on training and learning until you can't anymore! Understand me?"

"Yeah... I got it." Aaron is rubbing his cheek but looks at me with respect. Good. I got through to him. I turn and look at my other classmates. Samie and Jared are laughing at me. The other sophomores and the freshmen look at me in awe and respect. I half expect them to start bowing. Finally, I look at Jaci. He looks proud of me. I smile.

"We have got like an hour until dinner time; I would suggest finding random things for your pack, like earplugs. They saved my life today." I say.

Everyone but Jaci and I scramble around, looking in every nook and cranny, searching for helpful items. Jaci and I sit on the couch and curl up together. I lay my head on his chest and I can hear his heart beat. This is rare, so rare, to actually feel *safe*. I'm actually *comfortable*. This is a new development. It makes me miss a soft life. If I had met Jaci before the Academy, however, I feel as though this would have never happened.

It's not hard to think: *What if my life had been different? What if I did just one thing different, how would that alter my life?* The hard thing is to accept the way your life is and to *be happy with what you have.* Someone, somewhere, has it so incredibly bad. Hell. My parents may have it bad. I have it actually kind of good. Sure, there are monsters intent on ripping my intestines out, but I live in a gorgeous place with delicious food guaranteed to me. Someone, somewhere, has to deal with monsters of humans, has nowhere proper to live, and may not get enough to eat. This damned Academy may be trying to crush my spirit but sometimes I believe that I'm better off from it. Imagine that, a life lesson from a killing machine.

Time passes, and I lose count of Jaci's heartbeats. It's comforting, to be so close to another. I snap back into reality. It's just about time for dinner. Good, I'm hungry. Jaci and I stand and pull on our packs, and equip our weapons of choice. "Hey kiddies, whose hungry?!" I exclaim.

The sophomores come rushing out, already all set, the freshman follow after them, scrambling to get equipped. They'll learn, very soon. You would think that with the death of 8 of them, this school isn't joking around. Jaci and I are the ONLY two juniors in the school. The whole junior class didn't take this seriously. They thought it was an acting troupe, and that the dead were in on it. They found out the hard way, I guess. We all stealthily head out of the common room and into the hallway, slinking down to the dining hall. We're all very hungry. We get fed twice a day, but they happen to be very large meals. We are allowed to eat if we have food. We just need to find it.

We get into the dining hall and walk directly over to our table. I hope that the freshman have learned from earlier. Tonight's dinner is French onion soup with a side of crispy chicken topped salad. It looks absolutely mouth watering. As always, I scan my food for any signs of poisoning. I quickly check Jaci's, too. We're all clear to eat safely tonight.

The soup is hot and delicious. The lettuce of the salad is cool and crisp, and the chicken is warm. I can't understand why the Academy feeds us such fantastic food if they know it could be our last meal. I'm not complaining or anything, I'm just naturally curious.

I eat this food slowly, savoring it. The warmth makes my belly happy. I eat well past what's comfortable, but not too much that it hurts. I know better than that. I kiss Jaci on the cheek and hold his hand. I know we're safe in the dining hall. I'm the only student that calls it the dining hall. Everyone calls it the cafe, but I think that cafe is too boring a word for this majestic room. I pour the leftover soup into one of the three containers that I have in my bag. I dump the rest of my undressed salad into another container with the chicken, and put my full glass of water in the third. Now I have a snack/emergency meal.

It may be weird but it's saved my life, a lot like the glow in the dark paint that I have stashed away somewhere. Everything I do and we everything I have done is for a reason and it pointed my life in the direction that I'm going. One day, I may be really glad I saved that food. Or it will go bad and stink up my bag. I highly doubt that, however, due to the fact that the containers are vacuum sealed.

I look over to Jaci, and he notices. He slips his spoon in my mouth, and once again I taste the soup. Believe it or not, that is an incredibly sweet gesture. Food, though plentiful, was still a rarity here. There are a few students throughout the school who are trapped in some lair, starving to death. We never know when a meal will be our last. Sharing even that one bite with me was a lot like him telling me that as long as I'm with him, he doesn't care what happens to him.

There is panic at another table, and I turn to see what the fuss is about. Two students have gotten into a brawl, yelling and screaming at each other, taking swings. It looks like sophomores, and judging by the fact that one is male and the other female, it looks like they're breaking up. They scream at each other for a bit more before the boy snaps. No, he literally snaps. Her neck, that is. A hush falls over the dining hall as her lifeless body drops to the floor, blood pouring out her nose. The boy looks horrified and looks at his hands in dismay. If there was a good reason, he's safe. If not then...

Through the doors sweep three vampires. They wear black cloaks that drop all the way to the floor and long hoods that cover their faces. That boy is screwed. The people at that table cover their food; they know what is going to happen. The vampires ignore everyone on their way to the standing boy. He doesn't even bother wielding a weapon, he has no chance.

Two of the vampires grab an arm each and pull them back behind the boy, exposing his whole torso. The boy hangs his head, afraid and ashamed. The lead vampire lifts both his arms slowly and lowers his hood. His face is pure white, his eyes a shocking purple. Without any expression, the vampire takes one hand and shoves it through the boy's chest. The crack of ribs being spread apart roughly is louder than the boy's screams of pain, which is cut off as the vampire tears his heart out of his chest. Blood is spurting everywhere.

The vampire lifts the dripping heart and extends his abnormal tongue, catching the drips of blood. The tongue almost resembles that of a snake's, but one pointed tip and deep gray. The dark red splashes against his tongue.

One sophomore freaks out, stands, and runs to the door. The lead vampire whips to face her and points. The other two vampires fly at her with incredible speed, catch her, and tear her to shreds. I guess they considered that fleeing from an attack. We, the students, have to sit and watch in horror until the vampires leave the dining hall.

Afterwards we rush back to our dorm wordlessly. When we get there, we slam the door shut. I lean against the closed door to catch my breath before walking into the common area where everyone is chatting in fear about the scene that had just arisen. "Hopefully, that will count for tonight's attack." I say to the group.

I had spoken too soon. No one replies but Jaci grabs my arm and pulls me close to him. I turn and face the door, what I see there makes me get ready to fight at record speed. There, where I had been standing moments before was our very first daily haunt.

Chapter 4

It looks like someone has broken a rule. It could have been me and Jaci saving those sophomores from their own trouble... I doubt it though. That wasn't the first time. I'd helped save a bunch of students from their daily haunt.

To explain what a daily haunt is- they are attackers that come back specially for you every day. They will slaughter almost everyone before you figure out the way to be safe. There is always something that you have to do daily to be immune to the attacks, untouchable by your haunt. They only come back at night time, after dinner, when you should be sleeping.

Our daily haunt is a ghost. He looks really freaky. His image phases between bright and dark, flashing at an almost dizzying speed. It's a man. He looks almost like an old pirate. There are chains on his arms and legs, clattering in a breeze that we aren't feeling. He has a really long beard, from which crawl spiders and roaches that puff into smoke the instant they hit the floor. His clothes are tattered, and a broken sword comes protruding from his chest. He has no eyes, just gaping, oozing black holes. His hands are partially skeletal. The moldy flesh peels back from his bones in several spots.

One freshman faints. The ghost roars in anger and speeds towards the boy at incredible speeds, grabbing him by the hair, lifting him. The commotion causes him to awake just in time to see the haunt pull the sword from it's own chest, and decapitate him. The poor freshman saw it coming. I feel bad for him. We were all warned that this school was not for the faint of heart. He really should have listened.

Now, with a ghost, you want to stay very far away from them. Luckily, I have my long bow. I hand my scythe, fully extended, to Jaci for a bit of protection. My scythe is 12 feet long and very strong. I take aim at the ghost, and shoot. The arrow flies through the air, BB tip glistening, looking pretty damn deadly.

To my surprise, the haunt roars in pain and clutches his singed arm, where the arrow had grazed him. I'm genuinely shocked. "Guys, use your BBs. You can't touch him physically; it would kill you to try. Just throw them at him." I call out.

Jaci actually listen to me, as well as Samie and Jared. The others are skeptical. Before the BBs can even be taken from the bags, however, the ghost races forward and uses his bony claws to rip open a sophomore's chest and stomach. His intestines fall out and spill everywhere. The ghost roars and rushes at me. I quickly cock an arrow and shot him. He pauses for a moment before roaring again in pain. To save me, Jaci throws an entire handful of BBs at the haunt. The ghost turns and slashes at a freshman, spilling his guts. Suddenly the haunt is under assault, BBs raining down on him. In agony, the haunt howls and flees the room. We're safe, at least for a little while.

"He won't be back until tomorrow night. We have a few free hours to somehow keep BBs physically on our person, to ward him off. Maybe we would keep a few handfuls in a pouch around our neck, handing from our belts, in bracelets. We'll find any way to keep him off. I'll volunteer to test the immunity theory." I say.

"No!" Aaron shouts. "You're one half of the juniors left at the school! We need you to teach us, and we know that Jaci over here won't be much help if you're gone! We need you; you've already saved the remaining lives so many times. I'll volunteer."

I start to argue with him, but Jaci interrupts me, "Heroic. Thank you. If this works, you live and so does everyone else. Okay? Now, we need to find steel mesh. It is very thin, but incredibly strong and the holes are tiny enough that the balls won't slip out, but big enough that the BBs will be visible in them." The BBs have to be visible; it fills the effect of the most powerful weapon against this haunt.

Emma walks forward, showing us a handful of steel mesh. "Found a supply of it," She says. "Right over here." She comes back with armfuls of the stuff. "There is enough for everyone to have two, if we put about 100 BBs in it. A backup, just in case."

Brilliant! I take the handfuls and lay it out. "Okay, watch how to do this. I'll teach you how to make pouches." I take a piece, remove my dagger, and cut a piece. "You want a circular piece, if you use anything but you'll have those pesky corners that let the BBs out. Take some of the clear thread from your pack, as that is incredibly strong, and braid it with two other pieces of thread to make a small yet durable rope. Now, you're going to weave it all the way around the circle. You want to end up with the strings on opposite sides of each other. Then pull the strings so there is a small opening, and pour BBs in, then close off." As I'm talking, I'm also showing them how to do it. I pour 100-200 BBs. "You want a lot of BBs, enough to give off the vibe that you have them. You can make a loop with the leftover thread and put it on, say, your belt. That'll hold it to your person as well as keep the pouch closed." I do that, and show them my pouch. It is slightly smaller than a fist.

I had been very crafty before coming here; I know how to crochet and knit and such. Making a pouch is nothing, really, and it's nice to be able to show off my skills. "If anyone needs my help in making one, just ask." I say loudly as my other classmates get to work on it. I walk around and lend a helping hand, re-explaining the process to those who need it. In about half an hour, everyone is set. "Keep these with you at all times." I warn. "The haunt will be here every single night until you freshman are gone, but it can show up and attack you individually any time during the day. Remember to always tell who you're with to use the BBs if the haunt shows up."

My classmates nod. Jaci speaks "We're safe for the night. You can sleep, talk, bond, and do what you would like. Okay?"

I am tired. I am so tired that I just want to go to bed. Emma comes up to me and I know that I'm not going to get to sleep any time soon. "Will you tell us about your experiences here, so we can expect more?"

I sigh lightly. No sleep for me. "Yeah. My freshman orientation day, about 100 people drowned. Orientation is the first night, and it's always the easiest. We had a water nymph. Our hint was, 'I hope you know how to swim.' Some people didn't. What I did was as soon as I got my stuff, I put flotation devices in my pillow and I sewed some into my pack. I did this for Jaci too, that's how we became friends. I also stitched the fireproof material over my blanket at this time. I did the same for Jaci. He knows how to sew now, though, so I don't have to worry about him."

Jaci laughs at me and I roll my eyes. "The water nymph is light blue and mottled green. It can't physically touch you, like a banshee, but it raises water from below the ground. We all had to half run; half swim to the dining hall because the roof is so high. The water got higher and higher. Some drowned from tiring out, some from not making it to a room with high enough ceilings. It's good to depend on floatation devices in this instance because it can last anywhere from 5 hours to the whole day or night. I would suggest sewing flotation devices to the outside of your pack. It could save your life one day." I say.

"Tell us about the Banshee!" Calls out Aaron.

I laugh, "Maybe Jaci should tell you about that one."

Jaci rolls his eyes at me and takes my hand. We sit on the couch and he begins his story. "Reagan and I went down to the gym to train and work out because that is one of the best ways to pass the time. I'd highly recommend it. Anyway, just before we start, the floor starts shaking. It started shaking again, but this time we heard the shriek that was causing it. Reagan reached into her bag and pulled out two sets of earplugs, the really strong kind. When the banshee came in, we could STILL hear it. The sophomores that it had been coming after were on the floor, covering their bleeding ears. Reagan took one of her arrows, lit it on fire, and shot it at the damned thing. Banshees are destroyed by fire. Get this- the banshee blew out the flame with a shriek and the arrow was harmless."

The sophomores and freshman look almost scared. Jaci smirks, and continues. "So Reagan and I cross the gym floor, knowing that we can't physically touch her with our skin, and Reagan distracts her by being a threat. She takes her lighter and pretends to start lighting the arrow while I sneak around the banshee. Just before this haunt gets frustrated with Reagan, I light the night gown on fire. She doesn't notice until it's too late."

"How did you know it's a banshee?" asks one of the freshmen.

"We could tell right away by the inhuman shriek. Banshees are the only haunts that can attack in no way besides screaming. Their screams, however, can shatter things like walls and ceilings and floors. It will rupture your ear drums until you're bleeding out your ears, pop all the blood vessels in your head, then make your eyes explode. We saved the boys just after they started bleeding out the ears. With earplugs, you get a vicious ringing in your ears and a headache. They are always female, normally in tattered night gowns or a dress of some kind. They hover about a foot off the ground. Their faces are *always* covered. If you find a banshee with their face uncovered, you are utterly out of luck." I tell them.

They all seem really interested; I almost expect them to pull out some paper and a pen to take notes. "Guys." I gulp. "I have some very important advice." I look around. "When it comes to an attack, it is fine to work together. But never, ever depend on anyone else but yourself to save you. Even if you're trapped, no one will come looking for you because the common assumption is that you're dead. You are your best asset. It is vital to trust yourself. Let go of all hope that this is a prank. Let go of any fear of dying. Those will hold you back. It is okay to trust someone but *never depend on them.*" I'm glad to see them nodding in understanding.

"Alright guys, I'm tired. It's time for bed. Light's will be out in the sleeping wing." Jaci says. Oh thank heavens some SLEEP.

"Me too! I am dog tired." I say.

Aaron snickers as if he knows something. I roll my eyes. I guess that even in a dangerous setting, boys will be boys. Of course, Emma is still checking out my boyfriend. What a woman, huh? I may be gruff but believe me I'm a big softie. I'll miss all these guys. Even though I only know four names.

Jaci and I curl up together in bed and the lucky goofball passes right out. When I'm tired, it takes me a little while and a lot of thought to get ready to sleep. I wonder where my train of thought will take me this time. I also wonder how this school is still going. Whispers have been going around that someone faked being dead to get out of the school then ran to the authorities, and showed them their wounds. Word in the halls is they were going to shut down the school and the headmaster killed them. Or that the police were all on the headmaster's side.

I want to know what will happen if the whole school rebels and storms the headmaster's office. Why hasn't anyone done that yet? I wonder if someone actually had and the whole school had been wiped out. Yeah, let's not do that. It's just interesting to wonder.

I will admit, I am so scared to not make it to graduation. I wonder what Jaci would do without me. I'm sitting here thinking and the other students slowly pile in. I can hear the snoring and soft breathing as they fall into a sleep that I wish desperately to be able to have. I just keep thinking to myself. I wonder what qualities you need to have to get invited to this school. Obviously you can't be related to anyone who has gone here before, so my children are safe. Thank god. I wouldn't want them to suffer through this. It seems cruel.

This school is very orderly, it's actually pretty incredible. Now that we have a daily haunt, we don't have to worry about tougher demons. Demons come after breakfast and after dinner. I guess it's so we work off the calories or something. Depending on how quickly the haunt is destroyed, you could have hours of free time or no free time at all. The haunt stays until banished or destroyed. The rules here are simple, and so is the schedule. You just have to learn and realize that this school is organized.

I don't know why I'm still awake but it's absolutely agonizing. I want nothing more than to sleep. Is all the stuff I see keeping me up, causing my insomnia? I kind of laugh to myself. The Academy is a real school, but I can't go to college after this. I want to be a author, I could write honestly about what I've seen and pass it off as fiction. Only a lucky few ever make it somewhere in writing, right? Chances are, all of those few were educated. All I have for education is middle school and demon slaying. The biggest hint to "Get out of here before its too late" is the fact that there aren't any classes.

I would have been normal, I guess. Had you ever wanted to be normal? Well that notion is a misconception because normal is just a setting on a dryer. That's a saying that I heard in middle school, don't quote me on that.

I finally....*finally*...start feeling that familiar and oh-so-desired drowsiness that lets me know that I'll soon be asleep. Finally. I'm able to succumb to the dreamless, restless sleep that's about to follow.

Chapter 5

I wake up groggily. I stiffen, and then stretch. Today, for some reason, seems like more of a sure thing than yesterday. I'm not entirely sure what that means.

I shake Jaci awake-again; I have a knack for waking up exactly when I have to. It's like having an alarm clock in my head. Jaci jumps awake instantly alarmed. I smile, and get up to go get changed. I walk back into the sleeping room as I'm finishing tying up my hair. Jaci is still changing and I yell "Alright guys, rise and shine! Breakfast is in half an hour and we don't want to be late!"

Some of the freshman jump out of bed, alarmed. The sophomores crawl out of bed, used to this routine and leave to go get changed. Aaron calls, "Shut up, *Mom.*" sleepily. I'm really tempted to smack him again.

"Fine, starve." I snap.

Aaron gets up slowly, "I was kidding Reagan. Chill."

"I don't want to chill because that requires letting down my guard. Get dressed. You'll be punished if you aren't wearing your uniform in the hallways." I say.

Aaron laughs. "Wanna watch me change or something?" He winks at me, teasing. He is just pressing buttons, but boy does he do that well! It was actually really starting to make me as angry. His attitude is fierce. It will serve him well here.

I turn and start talking to Jaci. "Today feels really significant. I don't know why, though. It kind of just feels like today is a big day, like something is going to happen."

"What do you mean?" Jaci asks. He is genuinely confused... damn it!

"I don't know..? I just... I don't know. But I do know that something is going to happen today." I answer.

"Guys... Let's go." Aaron pokes his head around the corner. It's good to see that he's taking today seriously, his weapons are sheathed and on his person. Good. This boy has a very strong chance of graduating. Heh. I'm almost proud of him.

I sheathe all my weapons and stride boldly out into the common area. "Let's go eat." I say softly.

The other classmates smile at me. Maybe we all have a chance of being friends. We walk into the hall, and it almost seems orderly. We're walking not alone, but beside each other. It's probably the best defensive stance we can take.

There are streams of other students running down the hall. One of them pauses and whispers in my ear, "It all ends today!" then continues running. What is that supposed to mean?

"Guys... I don't know if it is going to be safe to go to breakfast today. Everyone okay with not eating this morning?" I call back. We are paused; my other classmates are in a semi circle now.

Emma calls, "My stomach feels like it's being clawed out, I am starving. I can't go to dinner without breakfast."

There are some murmurs of agreement. "Alright," I sigh. "Just be careful. These students are all going to get in trouble, so let's show the head master that we're being good. This way we aren't punished too. Keep you weapons sheathed. Walk slowly and in an orderly fashion. As soon as we get to the table, sit quietly and quickly. Do not speak unless it seems that all is normal. I'll speak first. Okay? I don't want any deaths today."

The freshmen look alarmed, the sophomores look determined. Jaci looks almost eager. Does he know what's going on? I hope not, I don't feel like watching him be punished. Especially because he's been here three years, the headmaster knows him and what he's like so his punishment would be more personal. I turn and we walk in almost military fashion, until we reach the dining hall. During the procession, fiery creatures fly down the halls after the running students. They look like phoenixes! The creatures swoop down on a student, their feathers made of fire shooting out at all ends, and pick him off in their beaks. The student is screaming as his body catches on fire and then *shick!* His head is ripped clean off.

The sight even catches me off guard. I don't know if I've seen a decapitation before. It's really violent, really sudden. The body of the student is jerking on the floor as the blood evacuates his body. It looks almost as if he's having a seizure, but without the brain to do it with. I know that people behind me are trying very hard not to throw up and run. They trust me in this moment. They believe in me to get them safely to the dining hall. Luckily, very luckily, the creatures don't seem to see us because we're behaving. We follow the rules, and it saves our lives.

When we enter the dining hall, all the students are standing and screaming. I hurry us to our table and we all sit down, silent. The screaming students are chanting and roaring. "Get us out! Let us out!" This is a riot! These students are going to get us all killed!

I look around to each of my classmates, my alarm mirrored in their eyes. Pedro the troll comes out and serves us our breakfast. I hold up a finder, and scan each of their plates. There is no discoloration, no excess liquids, no granulation of any sort. I flash everyone a thumbs up, and with our heads bowed we dig in. Each of us knows to eat slowly, and we do. Once we all finish, Pedro comes back and hands me a slip of paper, then takes our plates.

On the slip of paper words are written. I didn't know that trolls could write! I read the slip of paper. The handwriting is extremely messy, but I can still read it. It says "Doing good, keep it up. Don't look up from the table. Don't leave. Headmaster is coming." I pass it around so everyone can read it. Each individual classmate looks me in the eye and nods, and we all look down. It doesn't take very long of waiting because soon a scared hush falls over the dining hall. *Click. Click. Click.* I've heard that cane before. It's the headmaster.

He clicks to our table. "Ah, look." His deep voice is terrifying. "I have one faithful group of students." He flicks out a pocket watch and lifts my head by my hair. He presses a cold blade against my neck. "What you do, you do out of *fear.*" He mocks me.

"No headmaster. What I do, I do to protect my fellow classmates. I've made peace with death and yet I've cheated it these three years." I reply.

"Give me one reason why I shouldn't kill you." Headmaster tells me.

"I can't. For all I know, I could be killed in the next twenty minutes. Why put off for later what could be done now?" I reply. I know I'm cutting it close by being so sarcastic, but I'm praying that my nonchalant attitude is working. In truth, I'm terrified.

He pauses for a moment. I hope he is genuinely shocked with my reply. I feel the blade leave my neck, and warmth where a thin stream of blood trickles out of the wound it leaves. "This table will not be punished today. But you must stay to hear my warning to the students." When he walks away, Jaci takes my hand and squeezes it. He is scared. He is pissed.

I turn and watch the headmaster enter the crowd. It is like the red sea. The students who were so angry before are now scared. One brave girl gets in his way, and crosses her arms. She says something to him and he cocks his head, listening. After a moment he stares at her, and she seems more confident. He looks like he's thinking. After another few minutes she looks uncertain. The girl still doesn't move. Lightning fast, the headmaster throws up his arm and slits her throat.

Calmly he steps over her thrashing body and continues. The parting between the students gets even wider.

The dining hall is dead silent. The only noise is the *click. click. click. click.* of the headmaster's cane as he walks. He walks up to the podium we have. His voice needs no microphone, it echoes around the room. He doesn't need a microphone because there is no noise to talk over.

"Well you have been bad, haven't you?" He starts. He may be old but his voice is terrifyingly powerful, so deep. "You have promised yourselves a new beginning. You stand before me, once an angry mob, but have been reduced to sniveling weaklings. I laugh at you." He looks around with contempt in his eyes, disdain strong in his manor. I shiver. "Among you are sophomores and freshman. The only two upperclassmen in the whole Academy have enough sense to behave and *obey me*. Shouldn't you always obey your elders?"

I squeeze Jaci's hand. The headmaster continues, "You promised yourselves a new beginning, so here it is. This year will be the hardest yet. Every class but that one faithful class will have exactly one hour to themselves during the day, and five hours per night. And, on any given day this year, I will call an assembly where you will all meet here, and be punished. You will not know when. Congratulations! You got your new beginning! Remember to obey my rules because *they are law*."

The headmaster slowly leaves the dining hall, utter silence following. Once the noise of his cane is gone, commotion is growing. People are chattering like birds. One brave boy grabs a sophomore from my class. "What are you doing?!" I scream.

"Punishment for being a goody goody." The boy snarls at me. Viciously and abruptly, he snaps her neck and smiles at me, blood coating the killer's hands.

"You're going to die now." I reply calmly. I take out my machete and throw it, catching him in the forehead. He drops like a fly. Emma screams. "My kill is justified." I walk around the table and pull my machete from his skull and wipe the blood off. I know that I'm right when the vampires enter the room. My heart drops, for a moment I think they're coming for me. They walk up right in front of me and snatch the body at my feet. They start eating it, blood splattering over everything, their teeth gnashing.

The lead vampire looks at me and lowers his hood. His purple eyes flash. *You are right, mortal. Your kill was justified, you will not be punished. A life for a life, you see. There is a balance.* The vampire was talking in my head! He raises his hood again and, leaving the mangled corpse at my feet, they leave.

Jaci ran up to me. "What the hell happened?" He demanded. "You and the vampire got into like a staring contest or something, and you looked confused as hell."

"I spoke to the vampire." I reply

"But you weren't even speaking!" cries Aaron.

"Vampires can communicate telepathically. Hearing their real voice would kill you. It instills a fear in your heart, strong enough that it actually stops your heart. Be careful of them." I say out loud, to basically no one. "Come on; let's get back to the dorm."

We walk back, and the walk is uneventful. We all sit on sofas in the common area, lounging around. "So. Does anyone speak more than one language?" Jaci asks, almost lazily. Emma raises her hand, and all of the sophomores do. "I would suggest that you do learn another, just in case you run into a Sphinx. Sphinxes speak to you in any language but your vernacular, or first language. They kill you by muddling your thoughts until you take your own life."

I glance around at my fellow classmates, calculating why we haven't been attacked yet. "Does anyone have anything bronze?" I got a few weird looks, before Jared hands me bronze dog tags that were around his neck. "Thanks, these are about to come in handy."

Just after I finish talking, Emma bursts through the door to the common area, out of breath. "Sorry!" she says. "I was attacked by a monster-like cat and it was so cute but it nearly ripped my face off!"

The whole class jumped at the sight of her, seeing that Emma was sitting right next to me. I look into her eyes, and I can't get over how stunning they are. So deep... deep as the ocean. Lovely sea green... I look into the other Emma's eyes, and they're the familiar brown. I grab my machete and walk up to her quickly, threateningly. My eyes are pleading her to look scared. I take the blade and run it across her hand, and blood starts pouring down. I put drops of her blood on the bronze dog tags. I wink, and back up. "Guys this is the fake! Get behind me." I cry out.

Everyone gets behind me, and I feel a hand on my shoulder. I turn to look, and it's Emma. She looks... unnatural now. I whip around and press the bloody dog tags to her forehead. She shrieks as black smoke comes off her forehead, and tentacles of black veins under the skin start spreading out. The skin starts peeling back, and dropping to the floor. The rest of my class looks on in horror, and soon the Siren is standing before me in its true form. What an ugly bastard. I take my machete and slit a deep cut in it's forehead, and it shrieks in anger, it lashes out with its claws and catches my arm. I wince in pain as my blood wells up. I move the dog tags down so the blood smears into the cut. The siren bursts into flame and shrieks, burning up until there is nothing but ashes and a scent of the sea.

"What was that *thing?!*" Shrieks Emma...the real Emma. She is totally freaked out, scared that something had impersonated her.

"That, my friend, was a Siren. It was the creature that had caught you in the hall and had bitten you. It had not intended for you to come back before killing us all, and then it would have killed you too." I answer.

Aaron asks, shakily, "H-how did you know?"

"I was wondering why we hadn't been attacked yet. In truth, I knew it had to be a shape shifter of some kind. It couldn't have been a werewolf because the eyes would have been silver. Emma's eyes are brown- a Siren always has the most stunning, deep, sea green eyes. They're like gemstones." I hand Jared back his dog tags. "That'll wash off... A bronze dagger would have been a hell of a lot easier but we were never given one. Giving us a Siren was sneaky. I guess it's true, this year will be harder. Anyway, you kill a Siren with bronze and the blood of someone infected by them. They are killed by their own poison. They are telepathic, too. Their venom makes you fall deeply in love with them that you would do anything for them, but Emma must already be truly in love to have not been affected too much. You saw it in its true form, ugly and hairless and gray."

Samie and Jared and Jaci look impressed, everyone else just looks scared. "Reagan, that wound you've got there is vicious." Jaci says.

"Yeah. I was infected with the venom so my blood would have worked just fine, but that was only after I had started using Emma's. The venom died when the Siren did." I answered.

"It didn't affect you at all!" Emma says, bashful. "You must really be in love." She glances at Jaci.

"Yeah... Love is actually pretty powerful." I answer. "Now guys, can we get the gauze? The sight of my tendons isn't exactly comforting."

Chapter 6

The whole class thinks I'm actually cool, and for the rest of the day we hang out in the common area, listening to my previous adventures and attacks.

"Did you ever encounter something that you thought was totally, completely freaky?" Aaron asks me.

"Well of course! Have any of you heard of a Wendigo?" I ask.

He shivers and says, "Yeah, I heard of them in an episode of 'Supernatural'."

"Explain what it is to those who don't know, please." I say back.

He gulps, and starts weaving his story. I have to admit, he is a fantastic story teller. "Well it's a North American legend that a group of people were lost with nothing but the clothes on their back. It was winter, and they were starving. One man in the group turned cannibalistic and started eating the other men in his group. Cannibalism was taboo, because people believed that you gained unnatural powers for eating others of your species. Well, this man had nothing still, so he would wear the remains of the others he had eaten to stay warm. Legend has it that the skin and bones that he wore became a part of him, turning him into this monstrosity. He had gained all the speed of the lives he had eaten, making him super fast. He also had their sight, he could see in the dark and 5 times better than an average person. He gained all their strength, so he could tear the flesh right off a human."

The rest of the classmates look scared and grossed out. "I fought one of those. The legend changes depending on region. Mine had been kidnapping students and holding them captive as a food source. Like banshees, the only way to destroy a wendigo is to light it on fire, or to put fire through its heart. This had just been after I made my bow and arrows. Each class had a wendigo, and each night one student was picked off. We were researching what it was and came up with the answer when we saw the claw marks. One night, it took Jaci. I tracked it to its lair under the school. I had nearly gotten punished for it. Using my lighter, I lit an arrow while it was tying up Jaci. Before the thing turned around, I shot it. It went right through him, close to his heart. I nearly caught one of the other students on fire in the process. Well he was *pissed* so he charged at me. These things are fast. I lit my shirt on fire and *hugged* him. He was in too much pain to attack, and soon he was dead but I nearly was too. I had to roll to save my shirt, and I am burned in strips across my back and stomach."

"That's incredible!" Gushes Emma.

"It's true; I was one of the students she saved. It was insane, she was legitimately on fire." Jared said. "Well it was insane until she got sick from the wounds. Didn't eat anything for 4 days, feverish... we actually had to go to the headmaster and beg for burn cream."

"He only granted it to us because he knew I was going to live but in agony for weeks. He is above torture, but not above murder." Jaci pitches in.

"Well that's a relief. But he let the wendigo keep the victims?" Aaron said.

"Because Wendigo do not torture, they store their victims until it's snack time." I add.

Emma laughs, almost nervously. "Who knew story telling could be so helpful."

I answer seriously, "Words are a very powerful medium. They can be wielded like weapons, or used like squirt guns. You can destroy a demon with words. Words are the only tangible portion of thought and mind. Have you ever tried to put into words what a color looks like? The color red is a fiery explosion of feeling and passions, making you feel physically warm and comfortable. You saw that color in your mind, didn't you? Story telling is just words, letters strung together to communicate an idea."

"You're really passionate about this." Aaron says.

"I've wanted to be a writer my whole life. I'm very imaginative, as a matter of fact the only reason I survived my freshman year was because I had thought that I was in a coma, dreaming all this. I felt like I couldn't really be hurt. But then, I was attacked and had claws raking down my leg. That's when I knew it wasn't a game. You know?" I ask. "What did all you want to be when you got older?"

"I wanted to be an auto mechanic." Says Aaron.

"I'm going to call you Axel then, okay?" I answer, laughing.

"I'll call you pen." He warns teasingly.

"I'll shove a pen up your nose!" I take out a pen and twirl it threateningly through my fingers. He jumps back slightly, alarmed. I smile and put the pen away.

Jaci chimes in. "I wanted to be an engineer. A chemical engineer."

Emma states, "I wanted to be a veterinarian. Or a nurse. I don't know. Someone who helps others and heals them."

"I wanted to be famous! A famous Youtuber." Says Samie.

"I wanted to be a singer in a heavy metal band." Adds Jared. The other, nameless students pipe in and I feel happy for once. We're all bonding, we're all safe.

"Everyone has their bb pouch, right?" I ask. "The haunt will be here right after dinner. Axel, are you sure you're still up for being the volunteer for this?"

"Yeah. Reagan we need you. You can NOT volunteer for this. No matter what. Got it?" Axel continues.

"I'm a fool and I've been known to survive interesting things. But fine. If this works I'm going to slap you for being idiotic enough to sacrifice yourself, and then hug you for being brave. Okay? But we have hours until then. So what are we going to do for the next few hours?" I ask.

"Tell us how you got so smart." Laughs Emma.

"Experience." I'm serious for a moment, but then I lighten up. "I was a total sci-fi nerd before coming here. Loved Doctor Who and Supernatural. Supernatural has actually saved my me a few times here, and it did certainly did today with that Siren. Hell, I'm expecting slender man to walk through that door any moment now and join me for a cup of tea. Always keep your mind open for the impossible."

"Stop sounding so damn Zen!" Laughs Axel.

"And the secret to life is happiness." I lift my chin and suck in my cheeks, impersonating a monk. That gets a solid, resounding laugh from the group. "Sometimes it is okay to be a glow stick-you may have to be broken once before you can shine!" The group quiets and looks solemn.

"Is that what happened? You were broken by some creature and now you shine as the star hunter in the school." Emma asks quietly.

I stutter. I'm shocked. "I-I'm not the best hunter in the school. I'm sure Jaci is better, or a sophomore. I just know how to pick up signs, and know way too much stupid, useless information."

"It's not so useless if it's saved lives, now is it?" Jaci asks softly. "Anyone in the school can say the same. You've saved just about everyone one time or another. Today was a fantastic example; no one else had even noticed that Emma had been a Siren."

"Do you speak another language?" I ask Emma. She shakes her head, no. "That's also how I knew. The chances were slim, but because no middle school teaches other languages. At least, not fully. I know that almost all of you know some words, the basics. Emma here just looks thoroughbred American. That's how I knew. Sirens speak every language in the world. Of course the chances were very slim, but I was right." I look around. "That makes me smart, not the best."

"Can I just mention that your sass at the lunch table was incredible AND it saved your life? If you had been sniveling and begging for your life, attempting flattery, you would have failed. The way that you didn't seem to care about your life, well, that was what saved you." Gushes Samie.

"That was my reasoning behind it." I laugh. "One can never be too at peace with dying, although I accept that it could happen at any time. It doesn't stop me from being scared, however."

"How many times have you come close to dying?" Asks Jared.

"Well the burning up with the wendigo was one. This morning with the headmaster was one. Um..." I pause to think. "I fought a fire imp once. That was weird; he burned his victims at the stake. Jared saved me from that one, my feet still hurt from that."

"Tell us about that!" Cries one of the unnamed freshmen.

"Well, you know it's an imp because they're about as tall as your hand. They don't shape shift. They bounce around like a bouncy ball, very hard to catch. They're generally a puke green color, with protruding teeth that are shaped like gravestones. They're ugly, and mean. There are fire imps, and ice imps. Ice imps, in my opinion, are much worse. They freeze your skin until you are blue, and then break pieces off of you while you're unable to move but able to feel. I don't know how that is but I can imagine that it is quite uncomfortable." I rush through the story, knowing that soon it will be time for dinner.

Jared notices the time too. "Hey guys, let's get ready for dinner and our haunt. Everyone have their BB pouches?"

Everyone checks, and everyone has them. I'm nervous for Axel. I hope that it works so we don't lose him. My stomach rumbles and I say, "Let's head out guys. Remember, keep your weapons sheathed unless you are attacked, or else you'll get punished."

I start walking, once again everyone in tow. Jaci walks up to me and takes my hand, squeezes it, then drops it. It is dangerous to be distracted at a time like this, walking through the halls. These halls have seen so much fear, death. These halls are worse than those of an asylum or hospital, where perfectly healthy and sane people die and go mad. The endless gray tiling of the floor and white, bloodstained walls are gory. The color combination is great, if not for the fact that it's dirty and bloody and disgusting. The footprints echoed off the walls, amplified and multiplied. I can see how students go mad here, taking their own lives.

Within a few more minutes, we arrive at the dining hall. It's was impressive, really. I sit down at our table. I wonder if a punishment was to be incurred here tonight. The headmaster is cruel, and he is pissed. The dinner tonight is pea soup-that was a bit of a punishment itself-and salad. The green color made it impossible to spot any poisoning, so tonight is a game of Russian roulette. If I die, then I die. If not, that's pretty cool.

I know it's a really bad idea to not eat something so I force the slimy soup down my throat, trying not to gag. I *hate* pea soup. I save the salad for last because it will wash away the taste of the soup.

I look around. Jaci has taken the same route as me and he's now munching on his salad. Two freshmen are eating; the others are slumped in their seats. Same for the sophomores. All those unnamed are slumped...are they dead?

I stand and check for a pulse in the freshman. Dead. Cold even, hardly any of the soup is gone. How the bloody hell did no one notice the demise of our classmates? I look around the dining hall; each table only has two remaining of every grade. Our class is the biggest now. What is this?! Is this part of the punishment?? Why are we being punished? My class has done nothing. This is a bit harsh.

There are tears on some of my classmate's faces, but they stay silent. Quietly, we take the pouches so we each have two. All that remains of my class is Axel, Emma, Samie, Jared, Me, and Jaci. One boy and one girl from each grade. I wished there was some explanation behind it, but I can't think of anything. We get up, still silent. Quietly we enter the dreaded hallway. We walk in peace and quiet. Once we arrive at the dorm, we find a piece of paper on our door, held on by a bronze dagger.

"What does it say?' Jaci asks dully.

I start reading it. "It says, 'Students. This is phase one of the punishment. I intend for the whole school to suffer. I hope you like watching your friends die. I also hope that you noticed that there is one boy, and one girl. In your grade, they are your partners. You must be beside them at all times. Once inside your dorm, you will notice changes. The punishments will be cruel, will be unusual. I fully intend to have the entire school dead before the end of the year, and then I shall leave. Not only will you suffer for your rebellion, your families will too. Enjoy your stay at this school.' Well that is just messed up. We have to find a way out."

"And soon." Says Jared.

We are currently sitting in our common area. "What did he mean that our rooms would be different?" Emma asks quietly.

"I have no idea. I'll go find out." I say. I walk around, inspecting. There is no difference in the appearance of the common area. The bathroom and shower are just as they always are. I cross the common area and enter the bed room. There are no beds here. Just six pillows. "What?!" I cry, indignant. The other students come rushing to see, and groan.

"It looks like we have work to do." Jaci says.

"Um... After we banish our haunt." Axel says, almost inaudible, from the common area. We run to the doorway of the bedroom before Axel puts his hand up, telling us to stop. There, in our doorway, is the haunt. Its chains are rattling, and he looks pissed. Axel looks scared. The haunt sees him and decides to try it. He raises his skeletal hand and brings it down with crushing force. I wince and just before his hand collides with Axel's chest, it is stopped. The haunt presses harder and embers of a flame seem to catch to the haunt's hand. He roars in pain, and presses harder and harder, before his entire hand is gone to ash. The haunt howls and leaves, and he will not return until tomorrow.

"Well... that was easy." Says Samie.

"Shut up!" I snap. My heart is still pounding. Axel could have lost his life. I walk up to him, slap him, and then hug him. Just like I promised. "Alright guys, let's build forts." I walk across the common area and grab sheets of the fireproof material, and spools of the clear durable thread. I walk back into the sleeping area, Axel in tow. "Give me a lift?" I ask Jaci. He quietly does, and I tie an end strongly to a rafter in our ceiling. I walk across the room the short way, and Jaci lifts me again. With just a bit of slack, I tie the other end of the string tightly to the rafters and then double it, making sure it will stay up.

They get the idea, and the freshmen build a tent with the fabric, using the wall as one end. They kept the fireproof material spread open by pinning it to the floor with the extra daggers. We took one more sheet and made a door with it, one that we can tie open during the day. All the rest of the sheets go on the floor for a bit of padding and blankets. We grab a lantern, close the door, and revel in the creativity of our large tent. They want to take our beds? We make a safe haven.

Chapter 7

We have hours to spend in our warm, dark tent. It's pretty cool, and spacious. We're able to spread out and be comfortable. The tent is fireproof, which is awesome. I walk out of the tent and get floatation devices for each of our pillows. Better safe than sorry.

It's such an odd punishment, taking away our beds. What purpose does it even serve? I suppose it might be to keep us more on edge. It isn't working very well. "Guys, I am so tired. Let's get some sleep. Remember, stay next to your team mate or partner. We don't want any more repercussions." Jaci says. He extends his hand to me, and I take it. We curl up together and soon, we're asleep.

I had been kidnapped and locked away inside a deadly game. I wasn't the only one, either. But I was the smartest of them. We had to hide and hide well from our takers in this small room, if you were found or spotted you were slaughtered. I hid on the ceiling, having used the narrow space between the walls as my leverage, and hid on the wide rafters. From here, I was able to see what was going on in the room around me.

When hiding, one generally goes as low as they possibly can. The kidnappers weren't entirely human, they were very fast. Within a few days, I learned their habits. I knew when they would be in the room, and how much time I would have. A lucky few people remained, hidden IN the ground and surrounding walls. Soon, I learned where they hid the keys needed to escape. When, painstakingly, I managed to get myself and the others out the kidnappers didn't know. We ran the unfamiliar streets, looking for a way home. We decided to split up and go our own ways, but to get in contact with each other through email once it was all over. I was the only one who made it home.

I blink my eyes open groggily. One would think that I would be used to the darkness of this school, illuminated just by florescent lighting and candles, but because I had seen sunlight in my dream that was what I was expecting.

I wake up Jaci by kissing his lips. For once he wakes up relaxed. I don't know if that is necessarily a good thing or a bad thing. We go and get dressed in peace, and sheath our weapons. We walk back into the tent and I almost feel bad to wake them. They actually look peaceful, my classmates. "Hey, guys, time to get up." I say loud enough to wake them.

Samie and Jared are instantly alert, Emma is upset, and Axel is sleepy. "I don't want to wake up, I was home. Even if it was just a few hours.... I was home." Wails Emma. "I miss it." Axel, unsure of what to do to calm his teammate, pats her on the back. Emma glares daggers at him and I nearly chuckle. Those two are probably going to end up getting married one day. I'm counting on it.

"Guys, now please." Jaci says stoically. "We have to get to breakfast."

"What if the headmaster just kills us all off?" Samie says, moping.

I roll my eyes at her. "Then we're powerless to do anything but die. C'mon. It's better than starving."

"We have dried food in our packs." Challenges Jared.

"Seriously, guys? What if you get trapped somewhere for a few days? We have to make an appearance anyway. I don't think he'll be personally killing off any of us through poisoning unless we do something bad. I think he's just going to punish us. And if we die, then we die. Okay? Let's go." I snap.

"Someone is feisty today," Laughs Axel. "Might as well live while ya can, Reagan. Calm down, okay?"

"Yeah, why so uptight?" Asks Jared.

"Just am. Nervous, you know. I don't feel like being killed any time soon." I say softly. "Get into uniform, let's go." The rest of my classmates finally take the initiative to listen to me and exit the tent. I turn around and nearly run into Jaci, who is standing close behind me. I wrap my arms around him and bury my face in his neck. "Hey there." I mumble.

"You okay Reagan?" he asks, putting his arms around me and his chin on my head.

"Yeah, I'm fine. Just had a weird dream last night, is all." I answer.

"Oh, that's weird by itself. You never dream." replies Jaci.

"Because I stopped myself from dreaming. When I came here I knew they would all be nightmares. Who wants to just deal with nightmares? I would much rather not dream." I mumble.

"Hey, lovebirds, are you two coming? Come on! We've got to get going or we'll be late for breakfast!" Samie scolds. Everyone seems to be in an awful mood. Well, great.

I leave, holding Jaci's hand. We walk directly out of the dorm and I call, "Hold your partner's hand. That's that the headmaster intended."

"Ewww." Calls Axel, being rude. I rolled my eyes; he's probably in Emma's league so I don't know why he's being bratty. Dumb kid.

The hallway lights are flickering. Has it gotten creepier in here? My heart jumps. I'm scared. There's nothing in the halls besides us, no sound but the flickering of the lights, the dropping of some liquid, and our footsteps. I wonder what liquid is being dropped, and where. I'm antsy, and we just keep walking. In a few moments, something wet plops onto my head. I pause, reached my hand up and touch it. It's slightly sticky, and when I look at it I determine that it's blood. I raise one finger so my classmates know to not follow my actions, and I look up.

Well, crap. Above me are the sleeping hall monitors. That's why we always have blood everywhere in these hallways. Above these halls are the dead bodies of students who died in them, forever to haunt and kill those who disrupt the hallway peace, and disobey the rules. That is just absolutely freaky. The hallway is too dark to have noticed this before. The bodies are strung to the ceiling by ropes, ligaments, bloody rags. They seem to be sleeping, blood dripping from their orifices. Quietly and slowly I lower my head. I walk at my normal pace through the hall and soon, we're in the dining hall.

"What was it? What did you see?" Emma asks as we sit down.

"It was the freakiest thing. They keep the bodies of those who die here in those hallways... they're strung up to the ceiling. They seem to be alive too. Which is why they don't smell. They're dead, but alive. They're sleeping, and they wake when the rules of the hall are broken. I'm fairly certain they're the ones controlling the phoenixes. It's really messed up." I answer.

The class looks horrified and in a few moments breakfast is on the table. Its eggs and toast. Nothing is poisoned so we wolf down the food. We're here for all of about five minutes. "Alright guys, remember to be extra quiet in the hall. We don't want to wake the monitors." Jaci calls. We all stand and he takes my hand. Samie and Jared are already holding hands. Reluctantly, Emma and Axel take hands.

We start walking through the dark halls once again. We get about halfway back before a high pitched, loud sneeze ricochets through the halls. I turn silently, and Emma is horrified. A creaking is heard over head, a rustle, and then *whoosh!* I look up to see the mouths of one student open wider and wider until the gaping maw was as long as his torso. A freaky moan comes from his mouth, and then, a small puff of fire. As soon as the flame hits the air, it breaks into a huge bird of fire, angry. It screeches then rushes at Emma, catching her by the hair and dragging her, screaming, down the hallway. Her scream is cut off in a gurgle and the phoenix's cry. She is dead.

The phoenix comes back and enters the gaping mouth of the student, becoming a plume of flame again, then; nothing. As I continue watching, the flat gray eyes of the dead student flash and scan us. I hold tightly to Jaci's hand. Dirty, bloody ropes extend and drop from the ceiling, followed by a body. The body is Emma's. She looks as though she has been dead for months. The ropes hold her body horizontal to the floor. Her hair is singed, and hangs over her face in tangled knots and clumps. Her face is towards the floor before her head snaps up. A deep, gravelly, inhuman voice comes from her, even though she isn't moving. Her eyes are still flattening from having just been killed, and the voice sounds layered. It's distorted and warped and sends chills up my spine. *You are breaking the rules.* She addresses Axel. *Where is your partner?*

Axel cries in complete fear, "You were my partner! *You were my partner and you were just killed! Emma you were my partner! EMMA! YOU WERE MY PARTNER!"* His repetition doesn't seem to be helping him.

You will join the guardians now. Emma says, expressionless and unmoved. *Die.* From her mouth come tentacles, dripping slime. I guess she hasn't been upgraded to a phoenix yet. They wrap around his head and Axel screams, flailing his hands in an attempt to pry them off his head. The grip is tightening more and more until finally, with a sickening wet crunch, his head basically explodes. He drops and his head is in pieces, what is left on the body is twisted out of shape. About half his head is done. What he has is one eye, part of his nose, and his entire mouth. The bones remaining are crushed to form odd lumps and valleys in his head. More bloody ropes fall from the ceiling and start twisting around him, cocooning him, and slowly dragging him upwards. We just lost our freshman.

Emma is raised back up, dead as ever, and we walk hurriedly back to the dorm. I'm unsure if we're going to be late for our first haunt of the day but our first sliver of luck comes when there is no haunt rattling our bones as soon as we get back. We're all really shaken. Since when is sneezing punishable in the halls? The headmaster must have vamped up the sensitivity, so even the most human of instincts would be punishable by death. This whole partner thing has gotten out of control, too. Emma, in death, didn't even recognize the partner or classmates she had once had. What happened?

We all slouch on the couches, weapons equipped, just waiting for our haunt to burst through that door. *Click-click-click-click-click.* What sounds like heels is now just outside our door. *Tip-creeeaaaakkkkkkk!* Something wooden taps the door and is pushing it open, allowing the heels to walk in.

In comes the best dressed woman I have ever seen. A long, midnight blue gown barely covers her high black stilettos. Her hair is like smoke, beautifully spilling over one shoulder. Her eyes, such a vivid purple, shine at us. "So I'm being paid to kill children?" She asks us, in a velvety smooth voice. In her hand is an ebony wood staff, with garnets and onyx anointing the top.

"What are you, a wizard?" Laughs Jared. Idiot! Never mock someone who can and will kill you.

"I'm a necromancer." She puffs up, indignant.

"You realize here its kill or be killed? We're going to kill you before you can have the chance to kill us." Samie snarls. Brave.

The necromancer laughs, deep and rich. "Oh silly children." Her face turns dark and angry. "Watch yourselves die. Only the pure of heart can kill me! You're in a school for murderers. You're all as dark as me."

I look over to Jaci. It's times like these that I love that we can communicate without speaking. He is the only pure one here, so we'll guard him from attack and he can kill this bitch.

She's laughing to herself. "All I need to do is bring back the oldest female's head to be paid? Oh, easy! Why is there such a large sum of money on your head, children?"

Jaci smirks. "Because we won't go down without a fight." I'm trying to gather up the information needed to kill a necromancer.

Necromancers are like wizards; they can raise the dead from their sleep and wield them as a weapon. To kill a necromancer, you must be pure of heart. When the blood of a pure person mixes with her blood, it acts as poison. But, for this to work, her undead must also be under siege and losing. This is due to the fact that she ties her life force to the undead in order to bring them back. Those being killed weakens them. A necromancer can only pull a certain number at a time, depending on their amount of life force.

I whisper this into the ears of my classmates, and the necromancer is laughing. "I am going to be killing children. What fun! It's almost a pity; I could have used you as my apprentices, with souls that dark!" She cackles and continues. "Let's get this party started."

She starts speaking in Latin, unknown words, and raising her staff. We hold our weapons at the ready, and her chanting gets louder and deeper. It would be foolish to attack her now, because at this time she is invincible. The ground in front of her opens, and from it come the groans of the dead, all rotting in Hell. She raises her staff above it and like a puppet on strings a monster follows. She must be using her entire life force to control him, already she looks weak.

This monster is surreal, and his mouth stretches literally ear to ear. His eyes are gone, just empty sockets. He is incredibly tall, more than nine feet. He has to slouch. I extend my scythe halfway and give it to Jaci. It's blade was forged of pure silver. Silver is a purity metal, and the fact that it is unleaded makes it nearly impossible to beat. I wield my hatchet, intent on chopping off bits and pieces of this monster with her life force contained in them, then throwing them back into the pit of Hell that the monster had arisen from.

The monster roars and lunches forward. I swing my hatchet and it loses its hand, which I kick between its legs. It falls; the necromancer tries to grab it and misses. Jaci manages to sneak behind her and hide, ready for my signal. He slices the palm of his hand, wincing, but looks back up to watch.

The necromancer is pissed. She can't extend any more life force for the sake of killing herself, but she once again becomes smug as the creature knocks Jared over with the stump of its arm.

Samie has her mini machete wielded and rolls under the arms of the beast and jumps, catching onto the monsters neck, and cuts deeply into it with her weapon. She is showered in the thick black blood and the monster roars and scrapes its claws down her side. She collapses and Jared rushes over to her, and cuts off the monster's leg at the knee, and kicks it into the pit. Once again the necromancer dives for it and misses and she yells in anger.

I take my hatchet and cut off the other hand, then knee, avoiding those dangerous teeth. The monster is in agony now, and the necromancer still hasn't noticed Jaci. As I cut off the monster's head, Jaci slashes the throat of the necromancer and puts his bleeding palm to it, mixing their blood. The monster dies, taking the necromancer's life force with it. I, with the help of Jared, manage to push the body back into the pit, the head to follow. The necromancer is dying, and Jaci simply lets her fall into the pit wailing. The hole closes up and Jaci walks over to us, covered in blood, a hero.

Chapter 8

Can I just take a moment to mention how incredibly attractive he is right now? Jaci stands there, looking almost horrified, but that isn't what gets me. I'm talking about the glint in his eyes, knowing that he saved our lives, *saved my life.* The way the blood splatters up his arm; almost decoratively. He walked over to me, clutching his wrist with a vise tight grip in an attempt to make a tourniquet.

"Can we get some help over here?! Please?!" Jared is freaking out. Samie is in a pool of blood, unconscious.

Jaci and I rush over. I take her pulse, she's still alive. It's there but growing weaker. "Jared!" I snap. "Go grab some gauze. Quick! Jaci, with your clean hand, get me some rubbing alcohol." The boys scramble up and I lift Sammi's shirt halfway, revealing the puffy wound. I wince. There is ooze gushing out of it, and the cuts are deep. Jaci comes back and hands me the rubbing alcohol and Jared hands me the gauze. Samie is going to hate me for this but I take the rubbing alcohol and dump it directly into her wound. She jerks awake, screaming in pain, and Jaci and Jared have to hold her down.

The ooze from her would is coming out, leaving the wound, and killing the infection. The swelling reduces dramatically, until the cuts look like deep scratches. Which, I suppose, is what they are. The puss hits the ground and sizzles, evaporating like acid and leaving a burn on the floor. I wince, that must have hurt. Samie is gasping in breaths, "Reagan you freak, you wonderful freak what did you do?"

"Saved your life, that's what. Jaci killed the beast; I got the infection out of you. It must have hurt like hell, but it did the job." I answer.

"Yeah it hurt!" She widens her eyes. "Hurry up and put that gauze on, will ya? I need to shower."

"You can shower at the end of the day, after the dinner time haunt. This way you can heal up and rest a bit. Still got your bb pouch?" I ask.

She pats it, and I do the same. We all check, and we all have it. "Now you just almost died sweetie, let's go put you to sleep." Jared says. He picks her up bridal-style and carries her into the bedroom. I don't expect to see either of them for a while.

I turn to Jaci. "What you did was incredible." I say. "I'm proud of you. Now here, let's get you cleaned up." I lead him to the bathroom and turn on the water, mildly warm. I guide his hand under the stream of water, avoiding his wound until most of the surrounding area is clean. Once the warm water hits it he winces, then relaxes. I finally get a clean look at the wound and it is not pretty. The scythe is an incredibly sharp object-which Jaci hands back to me now-and has sliced through all the layers of his skin and into the tissue.

"You'll need stitches." I say.

"Will you do them for me?" He asks.

"Of course." Once his hand is clean, I lead him to the couch and sit him down. I go over to the medical cabinet and take out the stitches kit. I've done this once before, on myself, and it hurts. I sit on the couch next to him. "This is going to hurt, Jaci. I'm sorry but it's true. Because the nerves are damaged, however, you may be slightly numb to it. I'm going to need you to not move your hand. Here" I hand him a log of gauze. "Bite on this, it helps deal with pain." I take out the long, curved needle and thread the monofilament thread through it. I spray the anesthetics on the thread and on the needle, thoroughly coating it. This makes less friction on the thread, making the process easier, and it cleans the wound in the process so it doesn't get infected.

I hold Jaci's hand tightly, and look up at him. The gauze is hanging out of his mouth, and his eyes are determined. I take the needle and, as close to the wound as I can, slip it through his skin. He winces and bites down, stifling a moan. It comes through the other side and I pull it up, as gently as I can. I repeat this about twenty more times until Jaci's hand is closed. The nice thing about this thread is it dissolves when the skin doesn't need it anymore, so I don't have to worry about picking it out. I tie it off and apply antibiotic paste over it, then medical tape, then wrap his hand in gauze. "Don't scratch it, don't pick at it, and don't touch it." I warn, and then kiss it lightly.

Jaci pulls the gauze out of his mouth. "Thank you, love." I blush. It has pained me to push him through pain but it was better than watching him suffer longer. It would heal cleanly now, without too much fear of infection or even extremes, like amputation. "I love you, Reagan." Jaci leans in and kisses me on the lips with true passion, a warm feeling. It is probably the nicest, most comfortable and safe I had felt for three years.

We break apart when Jared clears his throat. "Ahem..." He coughs. We both blush and Jared smirks. "So... Samie is sleeping peacefully. I see you've got yourself stitched up there, Jaci."

"You're interrupting a moment." I whine. Jared snickers.

Jaci speaks, "You've really got to learn to appreciate the little things, in times like this. A nice kiss, a nice moment. It's something that doesn't happen too often. We could all be torn apart from each other at any moment but as long as you realize what you've got, you'll realize how strong you are. It gives you something to live for, to fight for, to die for."

"Well now I know what you see in him." Jared says, and then turns and goes back into the bedroom to do god knows what.

"That was deep, Jaci." I inform him, then kiss him softly again. We have all day to go by, and I hear Jaci's stomach rumble. "Want a bite or two of salad?"

"No, we have to save that, just in case." He replies boldly.

"I don't really care right now. You lost a lot of blood and you need to get your strength back. Here," I open by bag and bring out the container of salad. "Eat a few bites. A piece of lettuce, a piece of a cucumber, a tomato. Anything to help you feel at least strong enough to make it to dinner with a fighting chance."

Grumbling, Jaci opens the container and snags a mouthful between his fingers and munches on it. He glares happily at me, angry to waste resources but happy that I cared. A bit of color returns to his cheeks, that's exactly what I was hoping for.

"Now you should rest, mister." I say, pretending to scold him.

"Only if you rest with me." He says, and extends his arms. I curl up to him and put my head on his shoulder. Soon I'm dozing off. I'm semi conscious, so I believe that I'm daydreaming. I'd rather daydream than actually dream, anyway.

The bell rings. That means that class is finally over, time to head home. Jaci comes up to me and kisses my cheek. "Can I walk you home?" He asks.

I blush, Jaci's one of the more popular kids at my high school. "Yeah, of course." I say.

He takes my hand and we walk into the bright sunshine. Its spring and everything is growing. The sun is comforting, after a long day of learning. I'm at the top of my class here. We're juniors, and soon we'll be thinking about colleges and SAT's. It's all so average.

We walk up to my house, and my mom is on the porch with my baby sister. She is three. My mom smiles warmly. "Who's this, Rae?"

"This is Jaci!" I give him a little shove and shyly he says hello to my mother. He isn't normally shy, I don't know why he is right now.

"Why don't you come in? Do you want some lemonade?" My mom offers.

"Ah yesss!" Jaci says; suddenly back to his normal self. Mom takes my sister and leads us inside, where she has made lemonade. I

look around in awe at my house. It's cozy. It seems inviting. We sit at the table.

Mom questions, "Are you guys dating?"

Jaci says "Yes" at the same time I say "No!" Mom is smirking, and Jaci and I look at each other.

Jaci blushes. "What I mean is, ah, I was hoping that maybe you'd like to, um, go out sometime?"

I smile. "Wake up sleeping beauty, its dinner time." Jaci says. I groan. I was having a daydream that made life seem so stereotypical. It was nice. Except I don't have a sister. Well, I might now, I have no idea.

I get up and stretch out my stiff muscles. I must have been cramped into that position for a while, if it's already dinner time. I check that I have my BB pouches and that all of my weapons are equipped and ready to go. They are, so I take Jaci's hand. Jared and Samie do so in a like manor, Samie leaning on Jared so she doesn't collapse. She looks better, and food will do her good.

Of course, once again, we're in the hallway. We walk through it as quietly as possible. It takes slightly longer than normal, due to the wounded state of the younger female, and when we sit I look around. Every class is present but the dining hall is very sparse. Many died. Most classes have only one grade, the rest have injuries. It's scary. The headmaster is taking this way too far.

Dinner is served. Pedro brings it out and it looked fantastic. We are each given our own individual plates. In the center he places a huge roast turkey, and stuffing, mashed potatoes, salad, corn, and gravy. I drink all the water from one of my containers in my pack while the turkey is carved by Jaci. I stuff the container full of the turkey and seal it, squeezing all the air out. Now I have a good source of protein. The container is roughly the size of my hand and then some, and stuffed to the brim with turkey. I also stuff the salad container, and add some gravy to my French onion soup.

Now I'm good to start eating. This whole meal is the only way that I have of knowing that today is Thanksgiving. Wow. Time really flies when you're scared and being tortured, huh?

I stuff myself, and it's delicious. I wish I brought more containers; I would have gotten some of that stuffing. It was a fantastic dinner, surprisingly so. Samie and Jared are still stuffing themselves and Jaci is filling his new containers, just like mine. He had gotten them today, taken them from Axel's stuff. It's more important to have the food than the water, because we have water bottles back in our dorm rooms. They get switched out every week. Which is very nice, believe me. The headmaster doesn't want us dead in any other way then to be murdered. Not because of bad/no water.

I'm stuffed, and start internally beating myself up for it. We still have our after-dinner haunt to deal with. We don't have to deal with any real fighting, but I still shouldn't have eaten so much because moving is definitely going to hurt. I'll still be nimble, thank goodness, but I'm sure going to be sore from the effort.

We walk back to our dorm, cautious. A few other classes incurred the wrath of the hall monitors and were wiped out. I didn't want to see it happen and there was no way to save them. It makes me feel cold, very cold, but I suppose it has to be done. When we get back we have mere seconds before our haunt fazes through the door. We don't know of its entrance until it yells in pain. I turn around and see that it's trying to grab my arm with its arm stumps. They're melting down, ash falling to the floor. The arms look like they're internally lit by hot embers, and the ghost looks pissed. He roars and leaves, and I'm astonished.

"That was a really fast haunt." I say. I turn around and look at the rest of my classmates.

"Yeah, that is kind of startling." Jaci says quietly. "We should be on guard tonight, okay?"

"Aren't we always?" Huffs Samie.

"Uh, Sam. Go get some rest, okay? Or you can take a shower so you don't dirty the material." Jaci says kind of concerned.

"Oh!" Samie says, excitedly. "I'll shower!"

"Do *not* take off your bandage while you shower!" I warn. "The warm water press will be helpful." She nods and walks into the bathroom.

We're left to the three of us now. "So." Jared is awkward, leaning his weight on one side and scratching behind his head. "What now?"

I'm stumped, and I guess Jaci is too. "I have no Idea." Jaci pipes up. We go and sit on the couches. Jared sits alone, and Jaci and I sit side by side. I put my legs up, across his lap, and lean back yawning. "Someone is tired." Jaci giggles, and tickles me. I giggle and laugh.

"Guys be serious. We need to be on guard, we never know when something is going to burst through that door and take our lives." Jared snaps.

"Are you kidding me? Our lives would be a hell of a lot better if we could enjoy them, even for just a little while. You need to learn to appreciate the little things. We're trained warriors; we can be ready at a moment's notice. And if we die, then we die with a bit of fun in our lives." Jaci huffs. "Like I said earlier, it's all about the little things. You have to appreciate them, and you know we are the most serious people when the time is needed. Live while you can, Jared. That is the best advice that I can personally give you here. I've survived three years and going strong. Who knows? I could be graduating next spring. If I do then I will take many memories from here. I've learned a lot, Jared, and it's time that you let yourself learn now."

Jaci is really opening up and being more talkative. It's nice to see some of his personality, I like it. We sit on the couch quietly; Jared is chuffed about being told off. When Samie comes out of the shower, we decide to just head off to bed. In the tent, the air is warm and dark. Jaci and I fall asleep instantly, holding hands.

Chapter 9

We awake to something strange and new. I open my eyes and see warm, inviting brightness. While we had slept, people or creatures had crept into our room and taken off any and every board that covered our window. When I wake up, I'm bathed in *sunlight.* I haven't seen sunlight in years and my god it is beautiful. I wake the others up and for a few minutes we're just in awe of its beauty.

"Guy's let's get to breakfast quickly. I have a feeling that something is going to happen, and quite soon. I don't know if it's good or bad but my god let me tell you it's looking pretty good." I say. We all get up and go change, astonished by the beautiful sunlight. I can see trees, grass. I can practically feel the nip of the almost December weather. In the distance...there are people. *And they are all pointing at the Academy, with its new lack of window boarding.* I'm shocked too.

I go back into the bedroom and see that we now have little camper beds. Well that is just delightful, isn't it? I take down our tent and stuff as much material in my pack as I possibly can. I also add two water bottles and three more containers. Something feels really, uncomfortably off about today.

We sheath our weapons and creep into the hallway. The halls are bustling with life, brightly lit. I look up and all the monitors are gone. The hallways are completely clean, and look normal even. Students stand around in the hall, no weapons equipped, talking happily. "Where's my copy of the memo?" Jaci asks, laughing to himself. We're able to walk to the dining hall in bright peace, where I'm astonished to see we have no tables, but a very long buffet at the end of the room near the wide open doors, leading us out of the school. Students are sitting outside, shivering in the sunshine.

The headmaster stands behind the podium. Today is just getting stranger. He starts to speak. "Would all students please assemble in the cafeteria please?" The microphone is connected to a PA or something because soon the students of the school, so few in number now, gather in the dining hall. "As you all know," he continues. "I'm old. Today is my 62nd birthday, and I'm retiring. I have no heir, so I am shutting down the school and moving to some place warm, sunny. Ah, retirement village. No worries there. Now I know that you all want this nightmare of a school to be closed, and it will be! You all want to go home, too! Unfortunately, if I let you go home, you're going to spill the beans about my secret of this school, and that would ruin my retirement. We can't have that, now can we?"

I can feel all the hope in the student body draining. "It wouldn't be the first time!" Calls a student in the crowd. "They would call it hype; they would say that we're crazy. That's what they've said about every other generation of the students. They call it the lack of socialism."

The headmaster laughed. "It does feel rude to just kill all of you, doesn't it?" He scans the crowd. "I'll tell you what... My two juniors. You are free to walk out those doors and never have to come back. You're safe. My guarantee." He tosses the two of us yellow bracelets. They're the graduation bracelets. "Those are the last two in the school. As you know activation can't be turned off. They won't work for you if you're dead however."

I'm drooling. I want to take it so badly. I slip on the bracelet and Jaci does the same. The flashing red light turns green, letting us know that we're covered and free to go. It would get use through the gates of the school. "We'll take the bracelets" I say. "But we won't take your offer until we see how you do it." The bracelets are a guaranteed graduation. Nothing in the school could harm you in any way while they flashed green. I saw the headmaster's eyes flash in anger. He pulls on a heavy duty gas mask. Oh crap. I'm scared, even though the gas is unable to affect me. I'll breathe it in as if it's air.

The head master starts laughing as the doors close and seal. A thick, yellow gas starts pouring into the room, and I scramble to get Samie and Jared to safety. People are trying to use their clothing as filters. They haven't started coughing yet. I see the loading dock door, it is slowly sliding closed. I grab Samie and Jared and basically push them under the door. Jaci is trying to help more people, and I tell him that I'll stay with him until he comes. We run and slide under the door, just barely catching it. It slams closed and seals within moments of Jaci entering the room. Samie and Jared are coughing and close to losing consciousness. Jaci and I work together to open the garage door. He lifts while I hit the stopper, and the door slides open allowing the gas to pour out. Samie and Jared gasp like fish for the oxygen.

I look through the window into the dining hall just in time to see all the bodies hit the floor. The head master is no longer in there.

They are all swollen, their heads deep blotchy red. I watch for a few minutes more and when their heads explode, I nearly bite my tongue off. The headmaster can't know that I rescued two students. They are so shocked. It was so gory, bits of brain and skull and massive amounts of thick blood. I am gagging, and I duck down behind the door, out of view, as Pedro looks in. I can't trust anyone. Samie and Jared are invisible to his sight on the floor, and Jaci is as I am on the wall. To Pedro, there is no one in here, so he moves on.

"We have to get out of here." Samie whispers brokenly. Jared holds her, whispering in her ear.

Jared looks at Jaci and I. "Were you in on it?"

"*WHAT??*" I nearly scream. "You know us. We could never assist in the harming of other students. Jaci was out there trying to save even more students. Jared, Samie, you have got to believe me. We wouldn't do anything to harm other students, I swear. I spent three years protecting others, which is why I fully intend to bring you to safety. Beyond those gates lays safety. We can get there, with these bracelets. We can go now."

Jared looks suspicious and it really hurts my feelings. "Jared, right now I don't care if they're plotting to blow us up and sell us for dog meat. If they can get us out of here, then I'll trust them." Samie said.

"We can get you out. The gates will open and they close slowly, so you can run out while they're closing. The gates act as a field, as you know, and will protect you from the headmaster. It is the best chance we have of getting you to safety." I say. "We can get out through this garage right here. When night falls we can sneak out easily."

"No. I want to go now." Jared says stubbornly.

"Well that could be the death of you." Answers Jaci. "But fine." He continues.

I nearly panic. *Samie is injured, and in no condition to run yet. Sneaking would be the best chance we have, in case the Headmaster knows that we have them. He would see the gates opening and know that it is us leaving, but he wouldn't be able to force the gates to swing closed before Jared and Samie could get through. I guess I could see Jared's point, however, he has spent enough time in this hellhole. I just hope that his impatience to leave doesn't get him and Samie killed.* The daylight is still bright and Jaci and I walk confidently out into it, and it's bitterly cold. Samie and Jared creep out slowly, sticking low and to the shadows. We manage to safely make it around the building, through the shadows, and to the front of the school where people are still crowded, wondering what happened.

Jaci and I stride across the sunlit grass, bracelets flashing, and the gates open for us creakily. People stop to stare, confused as to why two students were graduating in December and why two other students seemed to be stalking them. We walk out and Jared and Samie bolt to the gate that suddenly swings shut in their faces, knocking them to the ground.

"Did you think you could just leave?" Laughs the headmaster, as he strolls across the lawn. His cane is in one hand, and a huge AK47 is in the other. The people back up, astonished.

"No! Don't hurt them! They're the only two students left alive, please!" I yell, grabbing the fence. "You can't just kill off an entire school!"

"Well *I did anyway!*" the headmaster is laughing. The people around me gasp, and Jaci grabs my hand. I look back to see someone videotaping this on their cell phone. Good. "Everyone is dead except you two, these two, and me! So! Did you like watching their heads explode?" He cackles with glee. "What an interesting gas."

"You are one sick person." Jaci says his voice low and angry.

The head master shoots Jared in the head. Blood is sprayed everywhere and most of the people run screaming. Samie is crying. "I know I am." The headmaster says, and shoots Samie in the head. "What are you going to do about that?" And he then proceeds to shoot himself from under the chin.

After the sick horror show that I had half anticipated, half dreaded, there are about four people calling the police. Soon half the town is here, freaking out about all the blood and brain and bone fragments that scatter the ground. The police arrive soon and so do my parents.

Jaci and I are immediately brought into a more private part near the gate for questioning. "Yeah, if you go into the dining hall right now you'll probably see all the blood that's still there from the massacre of the rest of the school. He had been slowly punishing us, dwindling our number. Originally my class was about thirty kids.

Then it was six, then four, now it's just me and Jaci of the entire school. We were the only juniors for the entire year; the rest of my graduating class was dead."

"Will you show us where the dining hall is?" One of the police officers asks.

"Yeah, but just remember. Those guns won't help you in the slightest. Here." I hand one of the police officers a machete, the other a hatchet. Jaci hands the third one his hatchet, the fourth his scythe.

"Why do you guys have these weapons??" The police officers are shocked.

"To kill the monsters. It was kill or be killed. Some were poisoned by eating; most were killed by some sort of monster or natural disaster." Jaci answers. "Come on. Pry those gates open and *keep them open if you want to live, do you hear me?*"

As a team we march back into the school that we had just escaped from. We go in the way we came out, sliding under the garage door. Using my bracelet, I opened the sealed loading dock door. A wave of fresh blood scent hit us and the officer's eyes widen to saucers. Scattered, mangled corpses are strewn across the floor, missing their heads. A few of the monsters have escaped from where ever they were being held and are eating and drinking the blood and bodies of the carcasses. I see our haunt there, and Pedro, and one of the phoenixes.

The police officer says "Alright we've seen enough. Let's get out of here." We scamper out of the building as fast as we can and make it back to where the police are stationed.

"Is it the real deal?" I'm assuming it's the police chief who asks, judging by his huge badge and silly hat.

"Yeah, it is disgusting in there and there are these...things." The police man says.

"One was Pedro the troll, one was our daily haunt, and one was a phoenix from the dead kids." I say almost tiredly.

"What the hell do you mean? None of those things exist." Snorts the police chief.

"Your buddies here saw them. They're not lies." Jaci says stiffly. Tough crowd.

"Well then explain yourself. Pedro the troll?? A daily haunt?? A *phoenix from a dead kid?* What are those even supposed to mean?"

"Pedro was the name for the troll that served us our food. He is an actual troll. Our daily haunt is a ghost who is allergic or something to BBs, and he comes back to try to kill us every day. The phoenix spawns from the mouth of the children who die in the school, they get strung up to the ceiling and they watch the hallways to make sure we don't break the rules. It's a simple system, a deadly game." I answer him with a bit more explaining.

"This is all so hard to understand." The police man said. "What you're trying to tell me is monsters exist and every student who left the Academy and came to us was telling the truth?"

"Yeah, basically. You can go in and see for yourself, if you'd like. Take some pictures before the monsters eat it all." Jaci said.

"How are there monsters? Do monsters actually exist?" One of the police men asked.

"I personally don't think so. I think that the head master created them himself, somehow. I don't understand either, they were just there." I say. "As a matter of fact I knew something was up today when none of the windows were boarded up and all the dead kids in the hall were gone. The headmaster gave Jaci and I graduation because he didn't feel like killing every single student, and then he gassed the place."

"Now how does that work, those graduation bracelets?" One of the police asks.

"They make us immune to anyone and anything in the Academy, as well as control the gate one time. As long as we wear them, anyone who intends us harm with any connection to the Academy cannot touch us. We could wear them our whole lives and be safe." I say.

"Now why did he give them to only you two?" The policemen are taking notes. Smart of them, it's hard to follow.

"We're unsure. Could it be because he had only two left, and there were only two juniors? Maybe in a way he didn't want to kill us? He wanted to see what his brave juniors would say?" Jaci was confused as much as I was.

"We're going to have to take you in for more questioning." The police officer says.

"Can we say hello to our families first? It has been three years." I ask. They nod and we turn, each to be embraced by what family has come and of course we're encased in questions and in love.

Chapter 10

"So...tell me again. This isn't some big, elaborate hoax put up by your school as a prank?" The police chief asks.

I rub my temples, my headache has been pounding. My surroundings don't help, either. I'm in an observation room, with one sided mirrors on either side, flat gray walls, hard tile, and a plain plastic table. It was boring in here. "People don't kill themselves for pranks. Entire schools don't get murdered."

"Don't be sassy, you're making this process go a hell of a lot longer. So why on earth would the headmaster just let his two juniors go?"

"My personal theory is he knew that we were the only two juniors in the school, and he claimed to only have 2 bracelets left. Maybe he knew that we were close enough to graduating, so he let us graduate but he also wanted to see us suffer so he locked us in with the children as they were gassed. He didn't expect to see that we had saved two students. He killed them, knew that his chances of escaping this were slim, and killed himself." I shrug. "Not too difficult to understand."

"Actually, yeah. It is." The police officer says.

"So...am I under arrest? Or can I go home and get some sleep because man I am tired." I yawn, proving my point further.

The policeman sighs. "You haven't done anything wrong that we can prove, so there are no technical grounds to arrest you. Go, get out of here."

I stand abruptly, "Where's my boyfriend? Where's Jaci?" The police man stands and leads me down a brightly lit corridor, with a patterned carpet, until we reach another observation room.

"Let him go." The man says gruffly. "They haven't done anything and they're tired. It's not exactly like they're a flight risk. They can come back in for questioning tomorrow. Plus, they haven't spent time with their families in three years."

Jaci flinches when they mention family. The man who was interrogating him stands and asks. "You haven't mentioned family; do you need a ride home?"

Jaci shuffles his feet, he's almost embarrassed. "My foster parents won't welcome me back... they were expecting me to graduate when I turned 18, a legal adult, so they didn't have to ever have me back in their house."

I'm shocked, actually. Jaci has never mentioned his family life, I guess. I'm just... surprised. "That is perfectly okay." I say. Jaci looks at me questioningly. "I don't think I could let you be anywhere without me yet. I've gotten so comfortable with you."

Jaci looks at me and for the first time since I have known him he looks scared. "Would...could I? Could I stay with you a while? Would your parents allow that?"

"Well let's go find out." I say softly. I take his hand and the policemen lead us to the lobby where my parents are waiting. I have a new baby sister; she's sleeping in my mom's arms while my little brother is lazily playing on his game boy.

"Oh! Done?" My mother asks excitedly.

"For the night." The policeman laughs, showing no real emotion.

"Mom," I interrupt the conversation. "Can Jaci stay with us for a little while?"

Her big eyes look at me, calculating her thoughts. "A boy...?" She seems worried, and glances at our hands.

I am exasperated, it's not like we haven't been together already. "The boy, who saved my life, watched my back for three years, who I trust, who I care about. I personally would be more comfortable to have him here, with me."

"But honey, doesn't he miss his parents?" my dad adds his two cents.

"They're dead." Jaci says, expressionless. I see the looks on my parent's faces change, suddenly they look sympathetic. My brother, Ryan, even looks up from his game for a moment.

My mom swallows her reservations. "Okay. I guess. Just...please. Don't get pregnant." My lips are twitching and soon everyone breaks out into a laughter that soon engulfs the whole company. It's a nice laugh, relieving us of the weight that was on our shoulders. I can feel the annoyance of the police and soon they leave us in peace. Oh, it is good to be home.

Thank *god* my mom has a minivan. There's enough room for everyone, which means no awkward squeezing. "Jaci, honey, do you want to swing by your foster parent's house and pick up your stuff?" My mom asks, as she straps in my baby sister.

His eyes brighten. "Yeah! They promised me they would save my stuff and not go through it." He laughs. "I'm just going to grab some clothes, my game boy and my games, and the money I've been saving up." He says to me. He gives my mom the address and she nods, and starts driving to that location. Within the next ten minutes, we arrive at a quaint little home with a few lights on down stairs.

"Do you want me to go with you?" I ask.

He shakes his head, "Nah, it can't take too long. Plus, they're really strict. Really....*really* religious. They'll take one look at you and judge you. I'll be out in five minutes, tops." He kisses me on the head and smiles. "Plus, I'm trained. You helped me train. I will be safe." He unbuckles his seatbelt and leaps out of the car.

My eyes are trained on him, watching as he knocks and is let in by an unseen someone. Even while my parents are asking me questions, my eyes remain on the door waiting for him. "So...you really were stuck in a house of horrors?" My mom asks timidly.

"Yep." I answer curtly. "I'm actually very, incredibly lucky to be alive. I saw a lot of people die, you know?"

"That's...terrifying." My dad said.

"Are you kidding?" My brother breaks in. "That's cool!"

I glare at him. "No. It's not cool. I saw people being torn to shreds. I saw people burn in fire. I saw dead children strung up from the roof. I saw my whole school explode. I saw two of my friends shot. Not cool." We sit in silence for a little while.

"It's been like 20 minutes." My brother complains.

Jaci has been in for a while... "I'm going to go looking for him." I say. I unbuckle my seatbelt and hop out of the car and walk out into the crisp air. It's very nice, the night sky. I walk up the driveway, hearing the crunch of the grass below me. My feet click on the wooden stairs of the porch and I knock on the door. As my knuckles hit the wood, the door creaks open, as if it were already open. I step inside and it is unwelcoming. There is no one here, but I spot a piece of paper on the table. I step over towards it and glance at it. I am shocked that it is addressed to me.

reagan.   my fosTer parents HavE taken   me awaY in Way tO get you to follow. NoT to fear, you Have to hUrry and pick a peRson To come Pick Anyone, REady to NoT come for the otherS.

I have no idea what this means. Maybe it means that they kidnapped Jaci, and had my parents kidnapped in a way as well. Probably surrounded. I was confused at his capitals, so I wrote them down in my head. *T-H-E-Y-W-O-N-T-H-U-R-T-P-A-R-E-N-T-S... They won't hurt parents.* They won't hurt my parents. I was safe to go after Jaci. In his own way he was brilliant, assuring me that my parents would be safe.

I have no time to explain, I have to go. I have to leave. I slink into the dark hallway. I walk into a room and instantly I assume it's Jaci's. It's blue. There's a Legend of Zelda poster on one wall, and a bunch of books are stacked around the room. It's impeccably clean in here, but there is one area where there was a sign of struggle. There are a few papers scattered on the floor. I pick one up.

Reagan. I expect something odd of my foster parents. They're acting differently, reserved. I'm writing this quickly because now I can hear them scrambling around in another room. I'm tempted to open the window and hide, allowing them to think I escaped. I don't think escape is possible. I can hear them talking. They have your family surrounded by sharpshooters, even trained on the baby. They want you to come out so you can come looking for me. They don't plan on letting you be with me anymore. What wonderful parents. They just don't like my girlfriend. Kidding. Anyway, you're smart. If you decoded my note chances are you're in denial. Chances are you came to my room and found this. They won't harm your family; as a matter of fact they're going to let them go as soon as you walk out the back door. I promise.

Anyway, I have to rush. They're coming. Please, come find me. They can't hurt me but being away from you hurts. And that's exactly what they plan. They're working with the academy so there is going to some sort of horrors. I don't know what to warn you about. But please, stay safe. His handwriting got sloppy as soon as he sped up his writing. I was lucky that the foster parents hadn't found the note.

I have to go. I have to hope that my parent's safety is ensured and I have to go before one of them comes knocking. I dash down the hall, letter in hand, and run straight out the back door. It's freezing so I run back in and snag one of Jaci's thick sweatshirts. I didn't know when I'm going to be back or if I'm going to be safe but I wasn't going to be back for a while.

Into the forest I run, with no idea where they could have taken him. As soon as I'm in the woods, I hear an engine start up. I turn back to see a white Corolla tear out of the shed. crap*!!!* Why didn't I see that coming? They wouldn't have taken him on foot! I run diagonally across the lawn and snag a bike. Soon I am riding fast, pedaling as hard as I can. My skin is absolutely numb, and I am just in time to see the Corolla make the turn. I follow them, and turn the bike just as headlights flood the street. Thankfully, I am out of view. My parents know now that I am not there, and neither is Jaci. They drive swiftly, pulling a U-turn and heading back to the police station.

I follow the white car as fast as I can. My lungs are burning, and tingling. My head is light and I am coming close to passing out. The Corolla leads me out of town, and just before I pass out it stops. I stop about 20 feet behind it, enshrouded in darkness.

They pull a struggling, gagged Jaci from the car. The house they lead him to looks normal, nice even. I creep around the back and spot a window. I quickly pry it open and slip inside, after hiding the bike in the shrubbery. The house, being new, doesn't give any tell-tale squeaks as I tiptoe up the stairs, looking for a hiding spot. It has to be a very good one; this wasn't a game of man hunt.

I slide behind a dresser. My frame is slim; I am a very petite, if tall, person. I hide in the shadows of the dresser. I think for a moment, it looks as if the house has been set up for a while. Did the headmaster plan all of this? Within a few minutes, the foster parents drag a semi-conscious Jaci up the stairs. I'm furious; I really want to take them down now. I don't have any weapons, the police had confiscated them saying that I wouldn't have to use them ever again. Liars.

They come back, just the two of them, after a few minutes. I suppose that they had put him in some room. "Locking him up would be inhumane." The woman said. As if dragging him here wasn't! "It's not like the girl could have followed us, anyway."

"Shut up!" The man snapped. "He'll be here in a few minutes with further instructions. Just calm down until then. Jaci is too drugged to leave. When he wakes up he'll want water and he'll drink what we left, and that'll keep him under."

These people are evil idiots. Why wouldn't I follow? I would have continued biking after them until my lungs burst from the effort. Who was coming? What was the grand plan to involve me in? There are footsteps coming up the stairs, and the foster parents become deathly silent. I can now hear a tap accompanied with the footsteps, and I'm getting angry. I swear to god if it's *him* some heads are going to roll. I am not afraid to decapitate.

Into the room walks a man in a very long trench coat, hunched over, his silver hair glistening in the light of the fire across the room. Silently I shrink deeper in the shadows. His deep, raspy voice sends shard of hate through my body. I would gladly lunge out there and snap his neck for the angst he has made me suffer, for the murder, for the pain.

"Do you have the boy?" He rasps.

"Yes. What are we to do with him?" The mother asks.

"Nothing. Literally nothing. You are not to talk to him, feed him, and see him. Not until the brat of a girlfriend shows up. He does not exist. And believe me, she will show up eventually. Once she's here, chloroform will work. Trap them; let them starve to death until they either eat each other or die of hunger. Just ignore them, they do not exist. While they are trapped, they cannot speak out against me and I can retire in peace." He says.

Now I know his plan. Now I know how to stop him. I have to get Jaci out. The fatal flaw is being unable to communicate with him, to see if he is still there. I would simply go and be with him until he wasn't drugged, and we would leave together.

The man says, "That's a bit...ah...never mind. We'll do it. You will make sure that we get a child? A baby?"

"Don't question me!" He snaps. Soon he leaves and the clicking goes away.

"Well... we have to do what he says... there is no connection to us anyway... We used fake IDs to adopt him in the first place. His foster parents are dead. What an extravagant plan." The woman sounds dead inside. Good. How could she hope to raise a child with the guilt of two dead teens on her hands?

"Yeah... Let's go to bed honey." With the term of endearment, I almost feel sorry for the couple. I guess they just want a baby. Certainly doesn't stop my sharp hatred towards the kidnappers. They go off, down the stairs, and ten minutes later I creep slowly out of my hiding spot. I move towards a closed, door, where I am assuming Jaci is being kept. The knob turns, and I enter slowly.

There he is, on the bed. He is out cold. I am angry and turn around to check if anyone has noticed that I'm slipping into the room. I am shocked and a rag is shoved into my face, the last thing I see is the teary eyes of a man, the foster father I assume, as he whispers "You shouldn't have come." Blackness engulfs my senses.

Chapter 11

I wake up the next morning, groggy and sick. I roll over and Jaci is awake, pale and very sick. I sit up quickly- bad idea. I fall back, dizzy. I guess I'm sick too. I'm thirsty, so very thirsty. I look over to the water, and grab it. I throw it against the door and it shatters, the water soaking up into the wood of the door and floor.

"Why'd you do that?" Jaci asks quietly.

"It was drugged." I sigh. "Your rescue really wasn't supposed to go like this. They probably locked the door. Shall we try it?"

"We have to get out somehow." Jaci replies quietly. I smirk. I'm just happy to know he's relatively safe. Well, as safe as he could be sick and drugged and in the hands of a crazy family. What little sympathy I had for this family from last night has burned, leaving me with just anger.

I stand up, very woozy. I feel light headed, but head over to the door anyway. I'm weak, but determined to get out. There are windows in this room, it's like an average bedroom besides the fact that we're left to our death here. I turn the knob, and it's unlocked. Yes! I would use this to my advantage. I take a piece of wire from a coat hanger in the closet and open the door slightly. I stab the wire deeply into the wood on the inside of the piece that the door uses to close, that way it's impossible for the door to close fully, so if they lock it we can still open the door. This means that while they sleep or go out I could get out and nurse us back to health.

I don't know how to pick locks, so my idea is the second best one possible. I close the door quietly and wobble back to the bed and flop down. "I made the door unable to fully close or truly lock. The outer knob will be locked but the inner knob will let us out." I tell Jaci. "We just have to worry about getting better."

"That's brilliant." Jaci said.

"Please, get some sleep. Are you comfortable? Are you cold?" I ask.
Jaci's voice is weak as he replies. "I'm cold..." I don't know what they gave him to make him like this. Something much stronger than my chloroform, my sickness is wearing off.

I walk over to him and I pull the blankets over him and kiss his forehead. He is freezing cold. "Sleep." I say gently. Jaci closes his eyes and in a few minutes his demure turns peaceful. He is asleep.

I pace around the room, checking it out and getting to know it. There is a desk in one corner, idiotic of them to give us so many weapon choices in that desk alone. There's a plush purple area rug near the bed. There are two chairs in the room, one rocking chair and one swivel chair. There is a stack of paper and a cup of pens and pencils on the desk. I walk over to the closet and see no clothes, just hangers. I am genuinely confused by this room; it's like that of a teenage girl. Or a young adult female who is home from college on the weekend.

There is one window. We are two stories up, so jumping would hurt like hell. I don't plan on breaking bones and being captured again, so that was a major "if need be" kind of situation.

I hear the doorknob turning and my interest is peaked. I whip around and snatch a pair of scissors from the desk. I hold them in front of me, yet ready to throw. The door opens and the woman peeks in. "I'm Jane." She whispers.

"You're the woman who kidnapped me, and her own foster child, in order to get a baby and you're going to watch us die. What the hell do you want?" The tone of my voice was icy; Jane knew not to deal with me.

"I want to know how Jaci is." She says quietly.

"Sick and dying thanks to you. I hope this is the room you raise the baby in. Then we can haunt him to suicide for your twisted ways. Then you'll be sorry, won't you?"

"I'm already sorry!" She said. "I want to help. But you don't understand! It's like a mule, either I get reward or I get punishment. My punishment is death, my reward is a child. Do you know how it is to want a child and be unable to have one?" Jane whispers coldly.

"Yes! I do! I wanted to have children one day, and you are taking that away from me. Why don't you just adopt a baby? How do you even know that the headmaster is going to actually give you the baby and not kill you? He will turn on you before you know what happened. I swear to you if I get out of here alive, then you won't." I say. I am angry, and it is conveyed in my voice. I hope she realizes the seriousness of the situation.

Jane slams the door shut and stomps away. Jaci stirs, waking up. "Reagan?" He calls out.

"I'm here darling. I was just talking to your mother. I don't think we'll be inviting her to the wedding." I say, trying to lighten the mood while rambling on mindlessly.

"Heh. You never said you would marry me." Jaci says with his voice breaking.

"It's that way with the person you're dating. You either break up or you get married." I say quietly.

"I would be honored." He says quietly.

I walk over and feel his forehead. He is absolutely burning up. "Go back to bed, please, until I can figure out how to help you."

Jaci is more than happy to oblige, and falls asleep instantly. I glance at him, worried for his health. He can't last more than a few days in this condition, especially without food or water. I make the decision to sneak out during the night to get him water and something to eat. Providing its unopened and such. I don't feel like having them drug us again.

I have a few hours to kill, so I sit at the desk and start writing. I have always loved to write, so why not chronicle my story? I start at my freshman year.

It all began with a letter. An invitation to attend a very private, very exclusive school. Rumor is people never leave the school. The headmaster of the school tells people that they got a job working at the school, so it seemed that they were never to be seen. What those who left, or "graduated" said, however, was completely different. It was like a prank. No way could it be true. What the graduating students said was there were monsters, murderers, demons, and every evil known. They said the students who were never seen again were dead.

It was the perfect ploy, of course. Who would believe monsters could roam the halls of a plain, if creepy, school? It was the prank of students, leaving and heading off to college. Those who left with bruises and wounds were told that it was because they were bullied. It was so few who left wounded. All left with these odd blinking bracelets.

Here I was, staring at the invitation to enroll at the Academy. Unfortunately, my parents had seen it first and they were excited. They wanted me to go. They believed I would excel, be great there. I, on the other hand, was scared. I believed the students, even if no one else did. I believed there was something weird happening at the Academy.

I was brought to the gates that fateful day, and was promised no classes and no outside contact. That should have, of course, sprung some concern with the all too eager parents. It didn't. The parents weren't worried when they were told it was going to be coed living. They weren't worried when they were told their goodbyes could be final. They should have been.

I could hear Jaci turning over the sound of my pen. I glance over my shoulder to see him bathed in the sunset light that's pouring in from the window above him. He is clutching the blanket. I go and look out the window. There is a neighboring house not too far away. A little girl is playing outside. I get an idea.

I walk over to the desk once more. The girl looks about 7, so she should be able to read just fine. I write *Hello there! My name is Reagan. I need your help. I've been taken away from my parents by bad people who live in the house next to yours. They took me with a boy, Jaci, and he is very sick. Will you help me please? Bring this airplane to your parents, please! I need your help. Hurry, please.*

I fold up the paper into a sturdy plane and force the window open. I fly the airplane and close the window, watching it sail lightly in the breeze. The sun turns it blood red and it lands a foot away from where the girl is playing. The girl is interested and picks it up. She sees the writing on the wing, and unfolds it. In a few minutes she runs inside quickly.

I keep looking out the window and the sun sinks in the air. It is gone, and the moon is rising steadily. Stars creep out into the blackening sky and in what felt like a minute, I watch an hour pass by while I wait for the little girl to return. She never does.

I'm devastated. I wonder if her parents care. I wonder if they think it's a prank. I wonder if they know about us, the missing children. I hope so. I can't bear the thought of being here much longer. I lie down next to Jaci. His feverishly warm body is shivering, as if he were cold. Uncaring of how sick he is, I wrapped my arms gingerly around him to lend some of my own body heat.

I wallow in my own self pity until its dark as pitch. The moon, so far along in its course, no longer shines into the room. I have to guess it's about 2 am. No one would be awake. However, I am not going to let my guard down. I grabbed the scissors once again and slowly creep to the door. Silently, I open it. I make sure to check my surroundings thoroughly and stealthily make it to the kitchen. The fridge lets off a low hum as I crack it open. It lights up to reveal a package of water bottles, about half gone. I snag two, and the visual difference is so slight that only a trained eye could catch it. I doubt that they had counted. I open the pantry and find a box of Ritz crackers, with three rolls of new crackers and an opened roll about half gone. I take an unopened roll. For good measure I fill a glass of water from the tap and drink it, so I can give more of the water in the bottle to Jaci to help him feel better.

I scour the kitchen and pantry, looking for foods to store that would be impossible to notice if they went missing. I took one banana from a bunch, the crackers, the water, a juice pouch, a handful of skittles placed in a zipped bag, and three clementines from the bag. It wouldn't last long, but it would last long enough to help Jaci get better. I sneak upstairs and decide I needed a hiding spot for all of this. I pry at floorboards, none come loose. I poke bricks in the wall at the back of the closet and find a hole, and fill it with the stolen food. The cavity in the wall was made by a really large bubble in the cement from when it had built the wall behind it. There was a few more inches of space left. Cool.

Quietly I put the bricks back in their right place and crawl back into bed with Jaci. I snuggle close to him, glad that I would be able to nurse him back to health. I fall asleep quickly because I am so tired. I don't dream.

When I wake up the next morning, I am greeted by the sight of Jaci's eyes. He is awake, but still very sick. "I'm so hungry Reagan."

"Don't tell anyone, but I stole some food. And some water. Want some?" I ask, already getting up out of bed.

"Yes!" He says, excitedly. "I think my body has been unable to cycle the drug through due to the lack of food."

"You're probably right." I walk to the closet, move the bricks silently, and as quietly as possible I take a small stack of Ritz and grab the water bottle. "Now this water is the only bottle that we have for the day. Drink slow. Here." I walk out from the closet and hand him a stack of the crackers. He takes a small sip of the water before putting a whole cracker in his mouth. As he chews, a bit of color comes back to his face.

The drug that they gave him had not left his system because he had no food or water to chase it away, making him sick. Now that he had a snack, the drug would finally be taken out of his blood and replaced with the nutrients that had come with the cracker. His body has needed those nutrients so badly, and now that he's was getting them the sickness is leaving.

He soon devours the crackers. "More? Just a few, please. Why don't you have some?" Jaci asks me.

"I want you to be healthy and strong again. This way we can take care of each other. This means letting you eat first." I walk back to the closet and retrieve seven more crackers. I give them to him and he stuffs one in my mouth. Automatically I start chewing. I make sure to chew very slowly so that Jaci eats the other six before I swallow mine. We both take a small drink of the water and I put it away, placing the bricks back in order.

"How did you do it?" Jaci asks softly. He looks so much healthier, and I am relieved. His voice is getting stronger, too.

"With the thought of getting you back up to health. Now... I need to go to the bathroom." I say.

"This poses an interesting problem...." Jaci replies.

"Lick all the food traces out of your teeth, brush off all the crumbs, and let's ask for a potty break. C'mon, pretend to be sick still and lean on me." I say.

Jaci does what he is told quietly. I wrap my arm around his waist while his arm is over my shoulder. I manage to take some of his weight for him and he droops his head. I bang on the door. "Hey! Can we get a bathroom break or do you want us to tinkle out the window and attract attention?!" I yell.

I hear someone stomping up the stairs and soon the man swings the door open. He looks grumpy, and says gruffly. "Come on, hurry up then." We follow him out and he ushers us to the bathroom. I let Jaci go in first and he stumbles in, what a great actor that boy is. After him, I go, and we are herded back into our room.

"What do we have to do to get some grub around here, eh?" I say, and the door is slammed in my face. "Right."

There is a little pebble thrown at our window. Ooh, what is this? I walk over to it and open the window, and poke my head out. The little girl is standing there, and she tosses up a crumpled paper ball. It takes a few tries but finally I catch it. She runs off quickly, disappearing into her house.

"What the hell? What does that say?" Jaci asks.

"Well, I sent a plane sailing into that little girl's yard last night while she played asking for help. It seems we got a reply." I say. We sit down and start reading.

Chapter 12

Hi Reagan.

I hope you don't mind, but I searched the names "Reagan" and "Jaci" on the news. You guys did indeed come up, you were kidnapped by Jaci's foster parents, right? I plan on helping out as much as possible.

I heard everything about your case; I'm actually going to call the police. As soon as my daughter, who is going to deliver this message for me, makes it in safe I will make the call. Police are probably on their way as you read this.

Is Jaci still horribly sick? Does he need medical attention? Well, I suppose there is no true ways for to you answer those as the messenger is back at home, safe. I really wish you well. There is going to be hell for those people to pay, I swear to you. Don't worry, you two will be safe soon. Thank you for reaching out to us. Glad to be of some service.

That is such a relief! It makes me feel really good to know that we're going to be rescued. I'm too sure about the police, however. It's said that the headmaster has connections in the police, allowing him to get away with operating a murder school. My hope is we won't be picked up by one of these supposed cops. That would suck.

"Jaci, we might be safe! This might all be over with!" I say joyously.

"That's so great!" Jaci says, excitedly. We sit down- me in the rocking chair and him on the swivel chair. Within minutes, I hear the crunch of tires outside and look out the window. There is an unmarked car pulling up, but a police officer gets out with his partner. Two more cars follow, each with two police men in them. There is an entourage of six policemen now, quietly walking towards our house. I wonder how many of them are on the headmaster's side.

The door downstairs bangs open and we hear shouting. Soon, someone slams our door open. It is a friendly looking police man. "Hey, you're safe now and we're going to get you home as soon as possible. Okay?"

I am more than okay with that, and I nod. The police man smiles, and gestures for us to follow him. He pulls out his gun and wields it, walking with us and making sure that nothing is going to pop out at us. Soon we are herded outside, where we see the "foster" parents being cuffed and shoved into one of the cars. The friendly police man lowers his gun and puts it away. "They won't be hurting you anymore." He says. "I'm Sergeant Nick Rockwell. You're Reagan and Jaci?"

"Yes! That's us." I say. "We were drugged but Jaci had it so much worse, he's still sick. Can we get a paramedic?"

"They're on their way. It's standard procedure to have medics at the scene of most crimes, especially kidnapping. It wouldn't have been called a kidnapping if your parents hadn't witnessed the car driving off, Reagan. Believe it or not, it's been nearly a week!"

I was shocked. So I hadn't been asleep for just one night... I had been out cold for days. Maybe I had it bad, too. Jaci sits on the steps of the porch, shocked as well. Soon the ambulance arrives, and we are taken into the back. Jaci is on a gurney, due to his state. I sit next to him. Both of us have an IV drip in our arm, and Jaci is once again asleep.

"So, what did you have to eat while you were there?" the medic in the back asks.

"Whatever I could steal for us." I answer. "They had planned to let us starve until we started going after and killing each other, because they couldn't physically hurt us. They had drugged our water so we also had nothing to drink. I managed to steal an unopened roll of Ritz crackers, and I had one of them from the pack. I gave Jaci a few handfuls to help him start to feel better. I also snagged a water bottle, unopened, from the fridge. This was all last night. Today is the first time we had eaten; I had only woken up yesterday."

The medic looks mortified. "Well this IV drip will get fluids back in your blood, as well as get rid of the drugs. Just a few more minutes of it and you should be fine. But you're malnourished. Here..." The medic digs around in the pantry and hands me a box of crackers. "I don't know when you'll be offered food at the hospital so you can take this. And this." He hands me two water bottles and an overnight bag.

I stuff it into the bag. "It would look a bit weird if I was going to stay at a hospital and didn't have anything, I suppose." The medic smiles. She's sweet.

"It should be another half hour or so to the nearest hospital, you were kind of out of the way. Sorry about the wait, but at least he'll get to sleep." She glances at Jaci.

"Yeah, thank goodness. He can sleep in peace for the first time in almost four years." I say softly.

"So it was true then, about the Academy?" She asks quietly. "Oh look! Your IV drips are done." She calmly takes the IV out of my arm, then Jaci's. She gives us each a band aid and gauze on it.

"Yeah, it was. It was all completely true. They say that the headmaster has buddies in the police force, in the hospitals, anything to keep him out of trouble." I say. It almost seems like I'm gossiping.

"Well I don't know the driver too well but he's been working with us for six years without any sort of suspicion. You should be fine with him." As she says that, the ambulance slows to a halt. "Are we here already..?" The paramedic says.

The door to the ambulance slams open and the driver points a gun at the sweet medic's head. *BANG!* Her blood and brains and skull pieces smear the wall behind her, I guess she had spoken too soon.

"Get out. Get lost. This is the only warning you get. You'd better hope you stay lost. The Headmaster has connections everywhere. If you're found, than you're screwed. I can't hurt you or I'd blow your head off. Scram. Don't ever show up again." He says gruffly.

I wake Jaci. "We have to get out of here." We walk out of the back of the ambulance, sullen. The driver doesn't notice my bag. We have to get to the nearest town. We start walking. I wonder what the ambulance was going to do with a dead medic and missing kidnapped kids.

I look around at the scenery. We are literally in the middle of the woods on a narrow road. This isn't all that pleasant. "How do you feel?" I ask Jaci.

"Much better. Thank goodness we got out in time." He says. I study his face, and he looks like he normally does. Good. "But now we're going to starve again."

"Actually, we're not. Not for a little while, anyways. The IV hydrated our blood as well as giving us full nutrients. It made us healthy again. We shouldn't need to eat for a while but when we do, the nice medic gave me an entire box of crackers and two water bottles. We can do it. We have survived worse." I say.

"I feel like a run away." Jaci laughs. We start walking back from where we came from. Not exactly a smart idea, but hey. Maybe it would get us into civilization.

It starts getting dark before we see a house. That it's just great. The house looks like something out of Cabin In the Woods. This is exactly what it is, but still. I look over at Jaci, and he glances at me. "Ah, no." He says.

"We need shelter." I say.

"I don't give a damn if we have to sleep in a tree! That looks like a murder house!" Jaci says protectively.

"What if they have food?" I say.

Jaci rolls his eyes. He is a boy and he does have an appetite, but I'm sure he values his safety more than his stomach. "If they have food, good for them."

I start walking toward the building. Jaci sighs loudly and follows me. I knock on the door and an elderly lady opens it. She is a nun. I smirk at Jaci, nuns aren't all that scary.

"What are you children doing here?" She asked, mortified.

"We were kidnapped, then rescued, then kidnapped again and we were dropped in the middle of nowhere and were told to never appear again. So basically, we're lost and very hungry." I say.

"Oh, goodness gracious!" The nun cries. "Come in, come in! Here, are you hungry? I was just making dinner."

We walk inside and the smell of meat fills the air. There is something off about it, it makes me feel sick. It isn't any kind of meat I've smelled before, which startles me. Jaci looks off, too. Good to know my instincts aren't failing me.

"Here, I was just about to sit down to some meat and soup. There isn't any of the meat in the soup however." The nun says.

"That is great because we were both raised vegetarians, we would become very sick if we ate it. That would be unfortunate." I say.

"Yes, it would." The nun says. There is something off about her, she hasn't mentioned God once. Isn't that their thing? I don't trust her too much but I'm unwilling to simply starve.

She sits us at the table and brings a crock pot of soup over. She gives us bowls and a ladle and we start serving ourselves. She brings over an oddly shaped hunk of meat. It looks oddly familiar.

How odd. We start eating the soup, after I search it for a trace of the meat. Not even the smallest sliver...good.

She starts pulling apart the meat in order to get some to eat. I'm half done with my soup and Jaci is drinking straight from the bowl, when she cracks through the meat into an area of ribs, lungs, and a heart. I know enough anatomy to know that it's human.

I stand abruptly, Jaci following my lead. "What?" The nun says quizzically. "Never seen a cannibal?"

"Oh damn that is nasty." Jaci said.

"Don't swear, boy! For that you get to help me eat your pretty friend here." She snaps. Ick.

The nun grabs her carving knife and stalks towards us. I don't have much time to think but I suspect that she was expecting us. She had made so much food-way too much for one person. Man, why is she even in a nun costume? This is just weird. She grabs my arm and I jerk away. I run, and Jaci follows me.

The nun morphs and changes into this screaming monstrous creature. It is almost like a werewolf, but keeps most of her facial features. Dark black fur sprouts rapidly from her skin, except a white patch on her head. That explains the whole nun bit. Her limbs become long, gangly, and disjointed. There is a cracking sound as her spine lengthens and she sprints at us even faster, quickly overtaking us. She roars and throws Jaci to the ground. Her teeth gnashing, he yells in fear as she lunges in towards his throat. I run at the creature, screaming in anger, and she lifts her head. From her jaws, nothing dangles. There is a look of pure confusion in her eyes, and Jaci has his eyes close and his head turned, scared but alive.

"You can't hurt us! You can't hire anyone to hurt us! We're protected from the Academy in every way!" I scream at her.

She slowly morphs back, fur once again becoming her nun clothing. "What?"

"The headmaster didn't tell you that he gave us protection?" I asked.

"He hired me to kill you." She snarled. "He would not be protecting you."

"You're not the first person he's hired to kill us. He has hired a few. One we killed, one pair was arrested and will be put to death. Do you want to join the string?" Jaci laughs.

She scowls. "No. Leave this place, now!" She snarls. Heh. We pissed off a werewolf thing. I couldn't wait to explain this to the police.

"Uh, got a ride?" I ask kind of making fun of the werewolf for its failed job. She hisses at me and points. My eyes follow her finger and I see a dusty motorcycle. Oh great. I hope Jaci knows how to drive one of these things.

It turns out, he does. He crawls onto it and starts it up easily. Poor motorcycle doesn't sound too sure of itself, but it sounds like it can run. Why is she helping us?

"Get the hell out of here before I change my mind. Go!" She snarls.

I crawl on the bike behind Jaci and clutch him tight. He does something and it roars, and soon we're off. He is fairly good at driving this, and I don't know how he knows how to drive it. Jaci slows the bike to a stop. "What are you doing?" I asked.

"I'm checking that the breaks work before something bad happens to us." He replies. Satisfied that they do indeed work, he starts back up and we roar down the road. We continue heading in the direction that we started from, and night falls heavily. The beam of light from the motorcycle is weak, as the dust filters it. After a while Jaci gets pissed, stops the bike, and cleans off the bulb. The light grows three times brighter and Jaci of satisfied, so we continue on our way.

We make it into a town labeled "Arevendale". I have no idea where this is. Literally, no idea. We park, and we run to the nearest house.

"Can you tell us what state we're in?" I ask urgently.

"A very disgruntled one! It's nearly 2 am! What the hell are you doing??" The man who answered the door says. "Hang on a second. You kids look familiar. Do I know you from somewhere?"

"We're all over the news, of course we look familiar! We were kidnapped!" Jaci snarls.

"Oh... You're Jaci and Reagan? Come in, come in." The guy says.

"Remember not to try anything. We are protected from any harm due to us by anyone who is in any way connected to the Academy. And if you're not, we were trained to kill and know how to out-smart anyone." I warn him.

"Yeesh. I'm not going to hurt you; as a matter of fact I'm calling the police right now. I'm sure you just want to go home and get this thing over with." The man says, and we walk inside.

Chapter 13

Through my experiences here in life I've come to realize that there are no monsters.

That's right. You heard me.

The real monsters here are people. There is evil, so much of it, and it is corroding the world as more people fall into its spell. Of course, I have faced off against some of the scariest creatures around but they're actually better than some of the humans I've met. They don't tend to fight for fun. They do it to make a point, be remembered, survive, and thrive, whatever it is. They're not truly evil, they're just themselves.

On the other hand, people torture others for fun, for a laugh, for their own sick pleasure. Some believe that they are justified. Some think they are heroes. They're not truly evil, they believe they're doing good. And then, there is the headmaster.

I know, it seems like I would think he's evil because I had been victimized. I had suffered his torture for three long years. But he didn't believe he was doing good. He didn't believe he was helping anyone. He did it for his own sick fun. He wanted to see if, when goodness snapped, did it kill? He made monsters out of the students he slaughtered, but none worse than him.

My train of thought is interrupted by a mug of hot tea being shoved into my hands. The steam wafts up into my face and I am delighted. I love tea. I study the steaming liquid thoroughly, although if it was drugged I would be unable to tell. I start chugging it down because I find no signs of poison. Jaci, having had the tea shoved into his hands as well, chugged it down when I did. We banged our mugs down at the same time and whipped our heads around to look at the man.

"What the hell." He laughs. "Thirsty? Hey, are you kids hungry?"

"Not particularly..." I say. Jaci elbows me in the arm and I go "Ouch! Okay, yeah, we are. We're always hungry."

"Why'd you try to refuse the food then?" The man smirks.

"Because the last person who fed us tried to feed us human meat." I say coldly. The man goes ashen.

"Hey, do you have a bathroom?' Jaci asks.

"Well duh! Down the hall, first door on the left." The man says. "While he's in there I'll brew more tea." The man scurries off behind me and starts bustling through things. Being the untrusting human I am, I switch spots so I'm standing, leaning in a corner of the dining room, and facing the man and the entrance to the hall.

"So it's all true?" The man says. "That is hella messed up. I'm Brian, by the way."

"Reagan." I say, calculatingly. "Now, when are you calling the police?"

"Oh my gosh how had I forgotten that?!" the man seems genuinely confused and concerned. He pulls a cell phone out of his pocket and dials three numbers. "Hello, I have the kidnapped children Reagan and Jaci here at my house. I'm at 57 Sumner Road, and I need immediate assistance. Thank you." He hangs up and continues with the tea. Jaci comes out, spots me instantly, and walks over. He takes my hand and Brian turns and says, "Aww."

"Shut up." Jaci sounds so serious, that he does. We sit in awkward silence while Jaci and I sip tea until Brian springs up.

"That's right!" He said. "Food!"

"I think it's a bit too late for that." I say as there is a knock on the door. I glance out the window next to me and see two police men, and one cruiser behind them. "That was quick."

"I live right next to a police station." Brian says. He sounds frustrated. I laugh at him. He walks over and opens the door.

"We're here for the kids." The police officer says, wasting no time.

"Yeah yeah, take them. They're bad company anyways." Brian says, and points to the corner where Jaci and I are standing.

The police walk in, and say into their walkies "Yep it's them, matches the photos perfectly." To us he says, "Alright kids, you're coming with us. Let's go."

"Are we finally going to go home?" I ask.

"No, we're bringing you back to your police department because now you have to be questioned about this latest kidnapping development." The partner says.

"Well crap. I am so tired. It's very early morning, I haven't slept in a while, and I have gone through a lot." Jaci said.

The police laugh. "Normally I'd reprimand you for cussing, but I guess you deserve it." I look at him, tired and angry, and the policeman falls quiet. Huh, never had *that* happen before.

"Let's go." The police officer said.

Jaci and I walk forward, still clutching each other's hands. I'm actually afraid to let go of him, that's what happens I guess. I am going to need countless years of very expensive therapy. Or, you know, I could just write books. Still expensive but hey, why not tell the world instead of one bland person? We walk out into the crisp dark. It's cold out, actually. Very cold. Is it still December? I'm completely lost on my dates and times. I thought December was supposed to be cold and snowy.

Oh well. I know I'm remotely safe. Hopefully these police have been out of the headmaster's wraith. I don't know how far his influence reached. As a matter of fact... "How long will it take to get back to our police station?" I ask.

The police men laughed. "You're two states over, hun. The entire New England received your photos and a warrant to find you. You're main witnesses in a huge trial of mass murder, and two counts of kidnapping. Who knows what else! You're really wanted, by a lot of people, princess."

"Don't call me princess, I don't take well to that." I snap.

"Whatever you say." He chuckles. He opens the door to the car, and I slide in. Jaci gets in next to me and I curl up to him. The back seat is tough plastic, and I am instantly uncomfortable. I put my head on Jaci's shoulder and look through the windshield as best I can with the bars blocking the back seat from the front.

It's hard, but I manage to fall asleep. Jaci is snoring softly long before I fall asleep, and listening to it calms me enough to make me feel safe. It's an uncomfortable sleep but it's deep, and I dream.

I never thought this day would come. The day that I have been dreaming of, when the world is so normal, when my life is so normal, that marriage could ever even be considered. Here we were, though. There he was, on one knee, holding the most simple and beautiful ring I had ever seen.

"Reagan, we've been to hell and back together. We've faced so many challenges. We've stuck together through it all. Will you marry me?" Jaci asks.

"Oh...my god. Yes!" I squeal. He slides the ring on my finger and it is a perfect fit. The ring is very simple, but absolutely stunning. At a straight on view, it's a plain silver band with a circle diamond in the middle. But from the side, the band is split wide with the shape of v's to add intricacy. It is absolutely beautiful.

Jaci stands and I wrap my arms around him in a tight hug and we kiss. As the kiss ends, I wake up. Hours have passed in the span of that short, girly dream. I never have dreams like that. I never even think of that. I'm not exactly girly. I smile softly though. I liked the dream, and I liked to think Jaci and I would last that long.

Speaking of Jaci, his snores have disappeared. I wake up more and we are STILL in the cruiser. Groggily, I look around. Jaci is staring tensely out the window, and I am concerned. "Where are we?" I ask.

"We're about four states away from home." The policeman who is driving says.

"Hang on; yesterday we were two states away." I say.

"We received a call while you were sleeping; it isn't safe to bring you home. It's rumored that the headmaster is lying in wait to attack you. We have to put you into extreme witness protection program."

"What the hell does that mean??" I ask.

"It means we're bringing you to Kansas." The passenger side cop says.

"Kansas? That's kind of random." I ask.

"That's the idea. We need to protect you. Even if that means making you new people. You're now a young couple, named Jason and Rachel Young, who are living together for the first time. We'll be giving you $10,000 a month. This will cover payment of the food and other bills. The apartment itself is paid for by the government and the FBI. You can't break cover; it could mean your life. You can't contact your family. All they know is that you're alive and safe. They don't know how, or even where you are. This is such a serious case that we can't take any chances." The driver said.

"How long will it take to get there?" Jaci asks quietly.

"The rest of the day, and into the night." He answers. I groan internally, I needed to eat and use the bathroom. The driver continues, almost answering my prayers, "Does anyone need a bathroom break? We can get breakfast, too."

"Yes!" I cry. He chuckles and pulls off the highway into the nearest rest area. I bolt to the bathroom and am happy when I am greeted with no line.

When I come back out, the police officer hands me a McDonald's bag. In it is a chicken BLT, and I am perfectly okay with this. There are large fries, and he hands me a coke. "Heh, I don't trust their hamburgers anyway. Thanks." I say.

"We were going to get doughnuts but that was too stereotypical." He laughs, and I like him. He has a sense of humor.

We get back in the cruiser and Jaci and I start eating our odd breakfast. Judging by the brightness, it's probably almost noon. The food sits in my stomach and I look out the window with Jaci. How the hell am I going to get used to calling him Jason? How long are we going to be in this protection program? What if this was all just a lie too? Is it bad that I'm so nervous?

Outside my window, the world passes in a sea of trees. Cars flash by, gone in an instant. It's a bit odd that we're still in a cruiser. "Hey, shouldn't we be in a normal car?" I ask.

"Yes, this is why we're changing cars at our rendezvous. Which is in a few miles, so don't worry; you'll be out of that uncomfortable back seat soon." The passenger cop says. He smirks. How would he know how uncomfortable it is? Is that part of his cop training? Is it bad that I'm kind of suspicious?

I look over to Jaci and solemnly take his hand. He squeezes mine and smiles at me, and I'm comfortable. Well, as comfortable as I can be sitting on hard plastic.

These past few days have been utterly nerve wracking. First, I watch my whole school explode. Then, I watch my best friend get her head blown off. Then, police questioning and Jaci and I get kidnapped. Well, he gets kidnapped and I get caught trying to rescue him. We are rescued, revived, kidnapped again. We visit a werewolf, nearly eat human meat, run away, and get taken by police into protection. No 16 year old should EVER have to go through this. It's just wrong!

I'm tired still, and rest my head on Jaci's shoulder. My eyelids drop and soon I'm asleep.

The tent was dark, but warm. The floor was hard, and I was certain that it was screwing up my back. I opened my eyes and was greeted with a velvety darkness. I stand, and walk out of the tent. The room is awfully dark, even with the incredibly weak light coming from the very tinted skylight. I could see the moon, jaggedly outlined. I loved the moon outside of the Academy but I was unable to admire it from inside.

I peeked into the tent and saw the masses of Jared, Samie, and Jaci. I walked into the common room and started sharpening my scythe. I don't know why I was awake, and I desperately wanted to sleep.

Within a few minutes I heard a slithering noise...isn't it a bit late for a haunt? I stand, and the noise fades. Almost as if something crawled into the bedroom. I stand and stalk forward, quietly slipping into the bedroom. By the weak light, I can see an alligator sort of creature creeping to the tent. It slips in before I could kill it, and my classmates start screaming. Something splatters against the interior walls of the tent. I bolt forward; scythes raised, and push aside the tent.

There is nothing inside except my peacefully sleeping classmates. I don't know what to make of this. I turn and the alligator is standing on two legs. It looks almost human-like.

"Beware of those you seem to trust." It speaks. Its voice is gravelly, like the scales on its body.

I have no idea what to make of this dream. It kind of terrifies me though, as I jolt awake. "Reagan, it's time to go. We're going to change cars now." Jaci is shaking my shoulders gently. I'm quite nervous. I don't know what my dream was supposed to mean. Were they talking about the police men? We haven't even seen their badges! I am such an idiot!

I get out of the car and confront a policeman. "I want to see your badges." I say calmly.

They smirk and pull out the cards. I study them very carefully, they seem to be legit. "It's okay to be nervous," one of the policemen says. "You've been through a traumatic experience."

"So, what about being questioned? Don't you need to interview us?" Jaci asks.

"For now, we need you safe. The display at the school is enough to detain this 'Headmaster'. Once he has been detained, we'll bring you back while still under protection and proceed with the trial." One of the policemen says. "Now c'mon, get into the car. We need to get going."

We walk over to a dark gray Toyota Corolla LE. It looks like it's a 2005 model. It's a bit old but it'll get the job done. I crawl into the backseat and sit in the middle, where Jaci sits next to me. I buckle up, and Jaci does the same. I turn so I am facing the window farthest from Jaci and rest against his arm. He puts that arm around my stomach and all this is done in silence.

Hours pass, and after eating from some burger joint, we drive through a sea of wheat. We pull into a town, then down a street, then into a parking lot for an adorable little apartment building. We are handed an envelope, "That's the money. You need all new things."

It was one *thick* envelope! "Okay." I say, accepting the envelope.

""We won't be accompanying you in, we really need to head home. Farewell kids, best to you." The taller of the policemen says.

It's dark, night time, but that doesn't scare me. The temperature is fair. We walk in and see a plaque with names and numbers. "James and Rachel Young........3B" So our apartment is 3B. I'm guessing that means third floor, room B. I don't know, we'd find out.

We walk up stairs. On each floor there are two rooms, A and B. We arrive at 3B and the door is unlocked. On the counter is a pair of keys to the house, and a bunch of paper and cards. There are credit cards, passports, birth certificates, social security numbers, and fingerprints for us with our pseudonym on them. I feel like a detective, or a double agent or something. I turn on the light. In the apartment, the bathroom is adjacent to the kitchen, living room right next to it. There are two bedrooms, and a balcony. There is a small table in the kitchen, and a bed and dresser in each room. There is a couch and a TV in the living room. I catch a glimpse of something silver, so I turn on the light. Someone is lying on the couch. On the floor next to him is a cane with a silver tip.

"Ah, children. You're a bit late; I was losing faith in you." I would recognize that deep voice everywhere. How the hell did the headmaster get into my apartment?

Chapter 14

Snow. It's such a pretty substance, for something so evil. It's evil because it's so damn cold, and there is not one thing I can do about it. It freezes my hair stiff, turns my skin red, and burns my lungs. But, it's so pretty to look at. It falls so daintily, so elegantly, it's impossible to not be awed by it.

Given my current situation, the snow paved streets of my home town seem like paradise to this warm, sunny death trap. I'm all for sun and shine but not with a murderer, all for heat but not for a killer. Here he was, though, tormenting us, hunting us. Like snow, there is nothing I can do about it now.

"How the hell did you get in here?!" Jaci is pissed.

"I am a very influential man. As a matter of fact, the car you were supposed to be in will be found in about a week, crushed to pieces with burned corpses inside, in a gully. You're welcome." He rasps, and sits up. "This is my retirement, you see. I need a part time job, however, so I'm babysitting supposedly dead kids. I hope you've seen enough of the sun to last a life time."

"Why are you doing this? Why don't you just leave? Take off to Russia or something, and just drop off the face of the earth without anyone knowing?" I ask.

"That would be too easy, and it would leave you unpunished. You ruined everything, so you really must be punished." The Headmaster says.

"You were the one who ruined it." I reply. "You gave us the bracelets."

"You weren't supposed to try to take Samie and Jared!" He cries. "If you hadn't, you would be at home right now. Safe. Instead of letting them die in quiet and secret, you ruined your own lives. You will live here, and when I die, you will slowly die here. You will be driven to madness with lack of food, water, light."

"What made you such a butt?" Jaci snarls.

"Hahaha that, children, is a story you don't need to hear." The headmaster says, and he stands. Taking up his cane, he leans on it the way he normally does.

"Let us go if you don't want to talk to us, you jerk." I huff. I'm really pissed, and rightfully so. Being kidnapped AGAIN is not exactly high on my to-do list, yet here I am.

"Everyone thinks we're dead, too. No one will come looking. Unless, of course, I planted a clue." Smirks Jaci.

"Yes, you do seem to be very good at that. If someone looking for you even enters Kansas, they'll be shot dead." The headmaster says smugly.

"You are one cruel man, you know that right?" I ask, spitting. "I just want to go home! Jeesh!"

"Can't do that. Sorry." The headmaster says, still smug.

Jaci strides over to him, way too fast for him to react, and sweeps the cane from beneath him so the headmaster falls on his back. He grabs the cane and presses it tightly to the headmaster's throat. "I swear to god I will kill you right now." Jaci threatens.

It seemed simple, so simple. Would the main threat be gone from our lives? Would we ever again have to be hunted down?

"Do it." The headmaster laughs. "Retirement, come early. Retirement from life seems nice right about now." Jaci hesitates. The headmaster laughs, "Too weak to defend you and your girlfriend from a life of pain. This is your only chance. Are you strong enough to save your own life? The lives of all the innocent people who I have under contract? Anyone who you know, like, and are even friends with will die if you don't kill me in this moment. I will make sure they die painfully."

Jaci's face hardens, as does his grip on the cane. He pushes down, and the smug look is wiped off of the face of the headmaster. "Go on!" The headmaster yells. "In truth, you will *always be hunted. By my spirit and my daughter, we will find you and make you beg for death!!*"

Jaci presses down, and the can makes a squelching noise as it goes through the windpipe. Bones crush in his spine and blood splatters us and the wall. When the cane thuds against the floor, the headmaster opens his mouth as a thin trickle of garnet red blood streams out. I just watched the death of my greatest enemy...again.

"We have to get out of here." I say.

"Yeah, we do." Jaci agrees. He takes the blood covered cane and pulls it from the throat of the headmaster, and we walk over to the door. There is no handle, how weird. I kick it, hard, and it doesn't budge. Fire shoots up my leg, and I am in so much pain. I clutch at my very sore leg and just hope that I didn't break anything. Jaci takes the butt of the cane and slams it against the door, and the heavy wood splinters. A shocked neighbor is walking out of her apartment next to ours and she gasps. "You're the dead kids!"

"We're not dead, but the headmaster is." I say quietly.

"That is a national story! You were thought to be dead, the police car flipped. How did you escape?"

"We were passed off from one guy to another, until we ended up here. The headmaster was inside, but now he's dead. We had to get away." Jaci says. "Please, do you have a cell phone?"

The woman hands it over silently, eyeing the cane with slowly drying blood on it. Jaci hands it to me, and I dial my parents. "Hello?" My mom answers, her voice is dull.

"Mom, Mom it's me." I say. "I'm in Kansas, I am alive. It was a ploy; they brought us to the headmaster. He's dead now, we killed him, but it isn't over. There's a contract on you and dad, and everyone. You have to be really careful."

"Honey, are you su-" her voice cuts off and I hear a bang.

"Mom?? Mom! Answer me!! What happened?!" I cry into the phone. I can hear a clatter; I guess the phone is on the floor. I hear three more bangs and I start freaking out. "Mom! Answer me!! Please!" I hear dull footsteps, and static as the phone is lifted.

A female voice speaks. "So my dad is dead? You killed my only remaining family, so I killed yours. Run, kids. I'm coming." The phone clicks off.

Tears are streaming down my face, and I cup my hand over my mouth. Jaci takes the phone from my hand and hands it back to the lady. She stands there staring at me. "What happened?" Jaci asked.

"They're all dead, my whole family. Even the baby, the newborn baby." Jaci wraps his arms around my shaking frame, and places his chin on my head. The lady gasps, covering her mouth. "I didn't even know my sister's name." I cry. "The killer told us to run because she's coming." I say.

"We have to get you to the police!" the lady cries.

"We can't, the headmaster tainted them. Nationally, I guess. We have to go on our own." I say, "Thank you for letting me use your phone."

"Is he really dead in there?" She asked, shakily.

"Yes, we crushed his trachea with his own cane. It's a bloody mess in there." Jaci says.

"Hey, why don't you guys come with me to the bank? Just to get you enough money to get out of here, and change your appearance so you can sneak out of the state unnoticed. Sound okay? Once you're well on your way, I'll call the police and report the body." The lady says.

"That is really kind of you." I say, shocked. The thick envelope in my pocket has completely slipped my mind. The lady starts down the steps and we follow cautiously. Jaci is still holding tight to the bloody cane, but now he is using it for his intended purpose. The blood has browned and hardened, so it lost some suspicion. The blood had streaked when Jaci smashed through the door with it, which also lost some of the 'holy what is that blood??' factor.

We made it downstairs and into the sunlight outside. It is funny, we were promised to never again see sunshine yet here we are. It's ironic really, that we manage to stay safe yet we leave a path of death and destruction.

We simply walk down the street to a friendly little bank, and the woman takes out $2,000 for us. "We really can't thank you enough." I say, and hug her. Jaci smiles politely, I guess he's not one for charity.

We went our separate ways and Jaci says, "Now we have $12,000."

"Ah, crap! I had completely forgotten about that! I wouldn't have taken her money if I knew." I say.

"We have enough to hide." Jaci said. "Enough to disappear."

"First things first," I giggle. "We have to dye your hair." Jaci stiffens, silent, and I giggle harder. "Come on; let's go find a Wal-Mart or something."

Jaci and I start walking, and in about an hour I am exasperated. "Can we please ask someone for directions?" I sigh.

"Fine." Jaci says. "Excuse me; is there a Wal-Mart or something nearby?" Jaci asks a random passing man.

"Yeah, go down this street, turn onto Freemont, and its right there." The man smirks at us, as if we were stupid. I'm really tired of people.

"Yeah, thanks." Jaci and I keep walking, and we make our way slowly to the Wal-Mart. We buy deep blue hair dye and bright pink hair dye and fake piercings. We need to look totally different. We also get heavy duty backpacks with camping hatchets, boxes of matches, pocket knives, clothes, and a few staple food items. It adds up to a couple hundred dollars, but is well worth it.

We're at the cash register when we hear this family talking. "You can NOT get your license from there, it is way too shady. They give licenses to anyone who will give them money, whether they knew how to drive or even have the right papers! No!" The mother is yelling at a boy about 15.

We cross paths and I stop her, "'Ma'am I'm a reporter, and I couldn't help but overhear. Would you mind telling me what DMV or school gives out licenses like that? I could write a story on that to put them out of business so the roads will be safer."

"Yes, it's R's Ed, down on Newport Road. Thank you!" The woman cries and scurries away.

I turn to Jaci, "We aren't going anywhere without driving. Who wants a license?"

"I have always wanted to drive. Can I get it?" Jaci asks.

"Go right for it." I say. We walk and as it gets closer to night we get to R's Ed. It's still open, so we go inside.

"What do you want?" Asks a grumpy manager. We're the only ones here.

"I want a license." Jaci says.

"$800 and it's yours." This was an easy bargain.

"I'll give you $1,000 if you teach me to drive too. All right now." Jaci replies.

The man looks interested. "Alright, do you have a car?"

"No." Jaci laughs. "All I have is $1,000."

"Cash?" The man asks.

"Yep."

That peaks the man's interest further, and he says. "Show me the money and it's all guaranteed." Jaci pulls out ten hundred dollar bills, and hands them to the man. "You must have been saving up for a while. Alright, follow me." All three of us head out back, and crawl into an old car. It's somewhat nice too, and starts right away. It takes an hour and a half but soon Jaci is a competent driver.

"Alright." Grunts the man, whose name was discovered as Richard, "Let's head back and give you your license.

We get back to the building and Richard takes a photo of Jaci, types in a few things, and in half an hour Richard plops a card in Jaci's hand. It's an official license and we didn't have to provide any papers for it. "Jaci Silva." Jaci reads. "Cool."

We leave, and Richard is counting his money. "I saw a car for sale by owner while you were driving. It looked pretty nice, and it couldn't be too expensive. Want to go buy it?"

"Yeah, let's go." It's about 7:30 at night, and that car could possibly be the only thing that we have to sleep in tonight. We walk, and it's 8:00 when we get there.

I knock on the door, and an elderly woman pokes her head out. "Hello! We're interested in buying the car you have for sale."

"Oh that's wonderful! I got it in my best friend's will, but I'm too old to drive it. It's brand new, and I'm selling it for $2,000." Her voice is soft and quiet.

"We'll take it!" Jaci says, and counts out the $2,000.

"What did you do?" The lady laughs. "Rob a bank?"

"No, it's part of our inheritance." Jaci says. The woman smiles politely and hands him the keys and the papers needed to let this be legal. She also signs a document saying that the car was sold to us. "Thank you!" Jaci said.

"No, thank you." The woman replies, and closes her door.

"Let's go." I say. Jaci unlocks the car and we toss our stuff in the back seat and get in the front. The car is a 2013 Dodge Dart, and it is absolutely beautiful. It's black and the lights are bright and silver. The car is brand new, and it's obvious by the purr of the engine and the new-car smell. Literally the best $2,000 I've ever spent.

"How much money do we have left?" Jaci asks.

I pull it out and start counting. "$8,872 dollars left." I say.

"Enough to get a hotel room for the night. How long did you say this hair dye would last?" Jaci is driving through the town, looking for a hotel.

"It'll wash out as soon as you shampoo your hair." I reply.

"Good. I don't feel like having blue hair for too long."

We pull up to a hotel, and pay for a room. I think this is probably our first time having a place where we can sleep peacefully.

We get settled and unpack our stuff a bit, feeling a bit unprotected without any weapons on us. I hoped that no one would attack us or find us through the night because we would be left defenseless. I didn't feel like being hurt tonight. It was so soon after we had obtained our freedom once again, I couldn't stand to have it taken away yet. Scratch that, I could not stand to have it taken away ever again. I would go mad, I have spent too much time trapped away in a hellhole of a place and I was never going back to the captive life again.

Chapter 15

The hotel room is kind of nice, allowing us to dye our hair. I dye Jaci's hair deep blue-brown, and streak mine with pink. I give Jaci a fake lip ring and he gives it a look of such disdain. "I'll put it in tomorrow when I don't have to worry about choking on it in my sleep."

I giggle, Jaci and I look completely ridiculous. "What's the point of this?" Jaci is moping.

"When people hide, they don't try to stand out. Therefore, we can get out of the state without being noticed by standing out like a sore thumb." I reply.

Jaci has his mouth agape. "Sometimes you're really stunningly smart. Stop it." Jaci then smiles at me.

"So long as we don't get ourselves killed in the process." I say back.

"Hey, are you hungry?" Jaci asks. "I am *starving*."

"Yeah I am, but we're going to have to rock a burger joint tonight because punks don't do things. It isn't socially acceptable. Or do you feel like take home tacos?" I ask.

Jaci is laughing, "Tacos all the way. Do I have to put on this stupid lip thing?"

"Yeah, I'd recommend it." I reply. "C'mon, there's a taco bell down the street." Jaci grudgingly slides his fake lip ring over his lip and I stifle giggles. He just looks so different from normal.

We get back in our pretty Dart and Jaci turns on the purring engine. We pick up a party bag of 6 tacos and 4 burritos...what can I say?? We're teenagers, always hungry. Once we're back at the motel, we dig in. I don't plan on being killed by a taco, and I don't plan on eating slow.

We eat through all of the food...every last bite. It has been years since I've had a taco. The Academy refused to serve them for whatever odd reason. It was an odd school to begin with.

"Well... there is literally nothing left to do. Bed time?" Jaci asks.

"Yeah, I suppose." I reply. I have to admit, I am kind of tired. I just want to sleep, I guess. I pull on baggy sweats and a sweatshirt, they are probably the most comfortable clothing I have worn in years, and I kid you not. The pajamas at the Academy were just a second set of tight clothes, just like our normal fighting clothes.

I crawl onto the king-sized bed and am in heaven. It's downy and the blanket is thick, if cold. I crawl under it and the bed sinks to meet my back perfectly. Jaci slides into bed next to me and I turn, put my head on his chest, and he puts one arm over my shoulder. With his other hand he reaches over and shuts off the light, throwing us into darkness. From the thin curtains comes a weak beam of moonlight, casting shadows along the far wall and comforting me in knowing *the whole world will be there for me when I wake up.* I close my eyes and smile softly, and for the first time I feel truly okay.

I was dreaming, I had to be. No way in hell was I walking down this street. It had been years, so many years since I'd been here. I'm truly home. I was in my birth town, walking down the street that I was raised on, and the place I'd known until I was 8 years old.

Orange Grove Avenue, what a pleasure to be back.

I guess I'm in for a pleasant dream. That old house, the one I'm staring at, has happy memories inside. The bad ones are hidden, tucked away, unable to be seen by even me. There was death in that house, of course. I moved away just a week after grandpa died. He had been really sick. Seeing the house he built, so many years later, and I miss him.

I walk forward, I have missed the Sunshine state. The tree shading the grass stands tall, rustling slightly as the wind jostles its leaves. The temperature drops as I step into the shade, out of the hot sun. I continue walking until I get inside the house.

It's exactly how it was when I left it 8 years ago. There is a partial wall dead ahead, and to my left there is the pet room. To my right is the table with which we were promised "elbow room". The half wall, the bar that was torn down to accommodate the new table. Where that wall stood is still abrasive. The living room, a step down from the dining room, was still painted black. It was an interesting color choice but watching movies in there gave whole new life.

The office, leading to the back yard, with all our encyclopedias. A cluttered desk sits in front of that bay window, looking out to where our pool is inflated with my favorite floatie. I touch the couch and memories flood back to me, my grandpa eating his ice cream and telling stories to me and my sisters. Stealing green beans from the pot before mom started cooking them. Getting rug burn on my palms and knees from pretending to be a cat in a freshly painted room. Giggling with my sister as we take over our brother's room while the blue and white stripped walls of our room dried, or helping mom sponge butterflies onto the purple walls of my baby sister's room.

I walk back out of the office into the living room, and cross over to take that step up into the kitchen, conjoined with the dining room. I remember when I had to take yummy bubblegum medicine every night, and I was so good about it that sometimes I reminded mom. The hall holds all four bedrooms, and one of the two bathrooms. My room was in the middle, my brother's room first on the hallway, my baby sister's last; and my parent's bedroom was right across the hall. I walk into my parent's bedroom and remember winning the giant Taz and giving it to them, even though I really wanted it, because I knew they liked him. I walk into their bathroom, with the glass hexagonal shower, and from there into the washer machine room. That led me back into the living room but this time I'm not alone.

"Who are you?" I call to the girl sitting on my couch.

She stands to address me. She is about my height but dressed like a hunter; sturdy black boots, tucked in flannel shirt, and light blue denim jeans. Her midnight black hair falls like smoke around her shoulders. "I'm Kate." She looks intimidating with her winged eyeliner, like she could kick ass and still look fabulous.

"That hardly answers the question at hand here." I say. "Who are you and why are you in my dream AND my childhood home?"

"I'm the daughter of the man you killed. I'm a huntress. I'm going to hunt you down." She says, her voice dripping with ice, chilling me to the bone. "And I am going to kill you."

"What?! He was a murderer!" I say. "I couldn't watch my friends die."

"He hunted demons!" Kat screams, getting heated. Her ice blue eyes are actually really creeping me out now.

"Actually, he turned the demons to us, watching as innocent students died on a daily basis, wondering if they would survive to kiss their mothers again." I spit in frustration.

"Then we're speaking of different men!" Kate is furious.

"No. I don't think we are and I believe that you know it, deep down." I say quietly.

"You like to ruin people's lives, don't you?"

"Actually, no. I like to save them." I reply. "I watched the heads of every student in that school explodes except the lucky four who managed to escape. Our numbers dwindled to just Jaci and I when someone shot the other two in the freaking head."

"Jaci." She sneered. "Men just suck in general. You seem pretty dependent on him."

"Hmm. Feminist to the extreme?" I ask.

"No, I'm just really gay." She laughs and I smirk, for a moment we are evens, matches.

"You actually seem really nice." I say.

"Doesn't stop me from wanting to hunt you down and slit your throat." She snarls.

"Woah. Feisty are we?" I laugh. "Come on, we talk about gayness and you're my pal but any other time you want to rip out my windpipe and feed it to me?"

"You killed my dad."

"You killed my mom, dad, brother, and new born sister. I didn't even know my sister's name. I killed a man who kidnapped us and intended to keep us locked up until we went mad. I went three years without seeing the sun. I have never seen a paler California girl than myself!" I say, desperate to have her see what I see.

Kate is quiet, and she says "There are things you don't know." She raises her arm, opens her hand and her palm is facing the floor. She raises her thumb, index finger and middle finger as if pointing in a punk rock way, and her eyes glow white. That same white light glows from her palm, engulfing me in it from between her fingers. She is silent, and suddenly my childhood home is gone.

I wake up and sunlight is pouring in brightly, shining on my pink hair. Jaci is still sleeping and once again I have to hold back laughter at the sight of his midnight blue hair. We sleep peacefully, undisturbed through the night and my first thought is that I would love a doughnut.

I kiss Jaci to wake him up and it works. He springs out of bed and into some Kung Fu position that is probably made up and looks around wildly. I roll out of bed laughing so hard that I bend over, gasping for breath. Jaci slowly calms himself down and looks at me, unaware of his goofy stance.

When he realizes, he stands up and brushes off imaginary dust, trying to collect himself and stop the giggle that I know is coming. Soon we're both laughing, hard, and it takes a while to control. I guess unlimited freedom does that to you. Why don't emancipated adults do this often? Do they?

"Jaci I want doughnuts." There, I came right out and said it.

"Alright than let's go." He says and grabs his keys.

"In our pajamas?" I question. We grab all our stuff, intent on leaving right away. We already paid for the room so there is no big issue to leaving like this.

He laughs, "Sure, why not? We can do anything we want. On the way, what was your dream last night?"

"Little does everyone know, I was born and raised in California and my dream last night was in that childhood home." I say as we're walking to the car. I continue with "It was exactly how it was 8 years ago. It was really cool, actually. I had missed that place. Anyway, once I took a good walk through the house and a long trip down memory lane, I met this girl on my couch. Her name is Kate, and she's the headmaster's daughter. One main point about her is she's 'really gay'. And I think she's a witch or something because she ended my dream in some sort of white fire that she controlled."

"Why does it matter that she's a lesbian?" Jaci laughs.

"It really doesn't but it was a turning point in our conversation, for sure." I laugh back. "She was blaming me for killing her father, who turns out to be the headmaster that we did actually kill. She got quiet and scary when I mentioned how she killed my whole family."

"She's the freak who killed your family?!" Now Jaci is mad.

"Pretty freak." I correct him. He rolls his eyes. "Ooh! iHop! Pancakes are always more welcome than doughnuts, anytime."

Jaci smiles, still reeling over the fact that in my dream I met a lesbian witch who killed my family. What kind of weird fantasies would that stir up in a boy's mind? I really don't feel like finding out. We walk into the iHop and I'm kind of happy to see that we aren't the only ones in pjs. We are the only ones with funky hair and fake piercings, however. I kind of cherish the feeling. I feel very punk rock. Woo. What do people do for fun anyway; stare at the weird travelers who are actually very different from anyone they should ever meet?

We sit down at a table and we're served menus and orange juice. That juice is absolutely gone by the time the waitress can even say her name. "Loretta". What a....southern name.

"Aw crap." I say to Jaci as Loretta walks away with our orders and after bringing me a new orange juice. "We should get a GPS before leaving state."

"Why?" Jaci asks.

"So we know which sunset we're riding off into, with our punk hair flowing in the breeze of the AC..." I say sarcastically.

"You are so adorable." Jaci laughs quietly. I smile and soon came our order. The mountain of pancakes with strawberry ooze on my plate looks too beautiful to eat, but that doesn't stop it from being gone in ten minutes.

Chapter 16

We finish at iHop and pay what we owe. It was certainly worth it. Pancakes are always worth it.

We get back in our Dart and head back to Wal-Mart. I grab an Aux cord and we get a GPS, a tom-tom. "Can we go back to my house in New England to get my iPod and laptop and a few other necessities?" I ask Jaci.

"Reagan, that is really dangerous." Jaci seems scared. He looks over at me and his expression is so serious that fires burn behind his eyes, New England is traumatic but to me home is home.

I'm slightly heartbroken. How am I going to scroll tumblr now? How can I get closure on my dead family? Does everyone think I'm dead? I suppose I can't just stroll back in... I'd never be allowed to leave again.

"So, where are we headed?" I ask.

"Anywhere you want to go." Jaci replies. "Anywhere besides home. We can go back in a few years."

"I am really bad at choices; I would have hoped you knew that by now." I answer.

"We need to get away from Kate, that's for certain. How about we go to California? That's basically on the opposite side of our world." Jaci replies.

I'm quiet for a moment. "Sounds like a nice idea but I think it would be obvious to Kate. Why wouldn't I flee one home to another?"

"You say that your dream with her was in your childhood home? Then we'll go, because she's going to think that you wouldn't go there, thinking that she would. It's a pretty good double negative and it makes sense if you really don't think about it. Okay?" Jaci says.

"Are you really sure that you want to do this?" I reply.

Jaci replies "Yeah, I do. You can show me your childhood town, school, landmarks, home."

I smile slightly. It's almost as if life is slowly rotating to be normal again. Of course, the death of my family was still a raw, gaping hole that would take years of completely separate therapy to get over fully. Going to elite, soul-sucking school was also out of the ordinary. But here in this car, I could hope for the best. Once Kate was out of our lives, well, maybe I could finally settle down.

I revealed a mixed CD. "I snagged this from my parent's car, and it's a CD that I made with all my favorite songs on it." I put it in the CD slot and soon, Mayday Parade was coming through my speakers. "Oh well, oh well; guess I'll see you in hell..." I sing along.

"You sing well." Jaci smiles over at me.

I just smile in reply and look out my window at the trees flying by along the side of the road, until we turn onto the highway. "Ready to escape the state?"

"What does that even mean?" Jaci asks.

"Toll booths have cameras; I'm sure someone who cares could very easily get the footage. Plus who knows what's going to happen? Dorothy was swept up in a twister here, you know." I reply smartly. Jaci rolls his eyes and smiles.

We drive a few miles before hitting traffic. "Great." Jaci groans. We sit in dead traffic for a little while before we hear it, the screaming. Something is booming, and it's getting closer.

People are getting out of their cars and running, screaming, in the opposite direction. I see flames licking the metal of cars in front of us and people, screaming and rolling, on fire. Jaci backs the car up slightly and, due to luck, is able to pull into the grass and zip in a break of the trees, getting us to the other side.

"What was that?" I ask loudly, scared.

"I have no idea but we've got to stay safe. Is there any other way to California?" Jaci replies. He is scarily calm and even angry.

"I have no idea." I reply.

"REAGAN AND JACI, I TOLD YOU THAT I WAS COMING!" a very high pitched screech rings out from behind us. *"DON'T EVEN TRY TO HIDE!"*

"Kate?" Jaci asks.

"I'm guessing." I huff. "Blend in."

Jaci slows the car to match traffic around us. He shifts over to the lane second from the first. There are loud thuds somewhere overhead, coming from behind us. We were the only car to cut sides, so I guess that kind of gave away our position.

There are two loud thuds on the roof of the car. "I hope that didn't just DENT MY CAR!!" Jaci yells.

Arms swoop down on either side of the car and open the back doors, and two girls slide into our car. Actually, slide is the worst word in the world for this. They just basically fall off the roof of our car; do a flip while in air which maneuvers them into the car, saving them from major road rash. I instantly recognize one of them as Kate.

"Drive. Get off on exit 14a. Got it?" Kate says.

"Why the hell should I listen to you?" Jaci replies to her.

Kate pulls out an AK47 and presses it to my head. "Is that at all motivating?"

"Fine!" Jaci replies. "That is a big freaking gun. Where were you even keeping that?"

"I pulled it out of your butt." Comes her snarky reply. "Just shut up and drive or I swear I will shoot."

"Kate, what the hell. I expected at least a day to hide from your little game. And who's the chick you brought with you?" I ask.

"That's Tess." Kate's smirk is visible in the rear view mirror. I can see the looks on some people's faces as they drive past us, seeing the gun. I think one couple pulled out a phone to call the cops, because Tess pulled out a pistol and pointed it at a passing car, shaking her head. "Speed up."

Soon we are pulling off at exit 14A. It's just fields after fields of wheat, standing tall and swaying slightly. The road turns from highway to narrow, one lane. It seems almost like a residential road. "Where am I going?" Jaci asks, exasperated.

"Take a left here." Tess replies. We pull onto a dirt road and soon, the road ends. In front of us is a creaky, old wooden house. The paint is peeling and all the windows are broken. The house is well hidden from sight, as if someone planted a square of trees around it to do just that.

"Out." Kate says.

I roll my eyes and I see a slight grin on her face. Why is she smiling if she brought us here to kill us? More specifically, why is she smiling at something I said? I just have to stop thinking about it. I'm about to be killed, I'm pretty damn sure of it. This is making me sad. I'm 16. "Too young to die" and all that crap.

We crawl out of the car and I snarl. "What do you want with us?"

"I want to punish the one who killed my dad." Kate replies.

"It was me. Now let him go." I say.

Jaci looks over at me and whispers loudly, angry. "What are you doing?" To Kate and Tess he says "I'm the one who really killed him. I crushed his throat in with his own cane."

Kate swings the AK47 between us, smirking as we try to defend each other. "Jaci, you have one chance to drive out of here unharmed."

Jaci looks at me. *It's like being handed the only two bracelets during our graduation. We were given the chance to leave, unharmed, and we took it. Is he going to go now?*

Jaci raises his bracelet. "You couldn't hurt me anyways."

"If what Reagan said is true about my dad, then I have no affiliations with the Academy. I could kill you both." Kate replies.

"That would simply be proving me right." I said. "Here" I toss her my pocket knife. "Cut my arm, and if I bleed you know I'm right. I want you to help us track down the monsters and kill these bastards." I extend my arm, face down, so that she can slice it without physically killing me. Of course, she makes it hurt badly.

There it is, blood streaming down my arm from the deep gash that she had made. "That really freaking hurts." I say. "Ow."

Kate backs up, dropping the knife in horror. "I-it's true?"

"Yeah, it is. That's what I've been trying to tell you. Please, you know the truth now." I say.

"Can we continue on our journey now? We've got lives to live. We're a bit young to be doing any of this, really." Jaci says, with an impatient tone.

"No, you can't just leave her like this!" Tess argues. I finally get a good look at her. Her hair is faded purple, with stunningly blue eyes. She's a short person, but dressed like Kate. They're nearly matching in clothes, besides the fact that Tess is wearing black skinny jeans and a fitted blue tee shirt with her combat boots. They are both fit, and thin, and it kind of makes me jealous.

"Why not, exactly? We're leaving, because she may be a mess but she killed four innocent people. For 'revenge'. She killed Reagan's whole family, including a new born baby, without getting answers first!" Jaci yells at her.
Tess goes pale. "You did what?"

"Please, don't be like that." Kate says. Her eyes shine with fear.

"You never told me that." Tess says with her voice scarily calm.

"I was angry! I thought she had killed an innocent man, one who had saved their life!" Kate yells.

"Well that's just a double negative right? Why would she kill someone who saved her? What would drive a person to kill?" Tess asks, than turns to us and asks "Why did you kill him?"

"Multiple kidnappings, keeping us at the school, forcing us to watch as hundreds of heads exploded from the poison gas he pumped into the dining hall, keeping us for three years against all sorts of monsters and horrors you could never imagine, and many attempts on our life along the way." Jaci lists off passively.

Tess's face grows more and more horrified, and Kate just looks sad. "What are we going to do about this?" Tess asks.

"We're going to stop these freaks once and for all." Kate is determined.

"Uhh...how?" I ask. "I've never really hunted anything, more like waited for it to hunt us and kill us."

"You're not dead so you'll be useful." Tess says. "C'mon, inside."

"Will you put that thing down already??" Jaci asks impatiently, looking at the gun pointed in our direction. Kate, exasperate, heaves the gun up so it is resting on her shoulder.

"I don't know what to make of all this new information." Kate says as we head in the creaky house. The wood splinters under my hand lightly, leaving wood standing up as if guarding against entry. The boards of the porch creak with every step. Sounding like rusty gunshots in every direction.

Once inside, the door bangs shut, making me jump. Kate laughs at me, asking "What are you nervous about?"

"Well maybe about the fact that I'm in some creepy run down house that I've never seen before." I answer.

"This was the best my father could afford." Kate says quietly.

"How?" Jaci asked. "His cane is silver plated gold tip with an ivory handle. The food he gave to the Academy was always top-notch. The school itself is gorgeous. He paid demons to kill us, too."

"That can't be true, because he always had a wooden cane when he came to visit." Kate refuses to believe us.

"I have the cane in my trunk, if you need to see it." Jaci said.

"Yeah, I think I have to." Kate replies.

Jaci and Kate walk out to the car on their own and I'm left with Tess. "So... how do you know Kate?"

"She's my best friend. She has a massive crush on me, too. We both kill evil crap for fun. I wish we got paid." Tess says shortly. "You're much different from how Kate told me you would be, and she never told me about killing your family. That crossed the line; we swore to never kill innocents. Not if we could help it. How did you know?"

"I was on the phone with my mom when all of them were shot, than Kate picked up the phone and told me she was coming for me, that I was next." I reply, my voice dead.

"That's kind of terrifying. Also kind of hot." Tess says. I groan and shove her shoulder lightly. She grins at me.

"I wonder what's taking them so long." Tess strides to the window and breaks out laughing. I run over and look out the window. They're just walking to the porch. "So you're the jealous type."

"Eh. I don't really like labels but yeah, I am." I say. Tess nods, and the door opens.

"How do I know this is really his?" Kate asks, continuing with whatever conversation they had outside.

"I don't know, don't you recognize it? At all?" Jaci argues.

"Kate, use you witchy power thing, the one you showed me in the dream." I say.

"What witchy power thing?" Jaci and Tess say in near unison. They then proceed to glare at each other.

"Yeah, I'm a witch. So what? It's come in handy, like when I tracked your butts down." Kate says defensively.

"Why don't you tell me these important things?" Tess yells.

"They're really not all that important." Kate shrugs off Tess's anger. "Besides, what does it matter?"

"We hunt crap like you!" Tess screams at her.

Kate is angry now. Without replying, she turns to the cane and raises her hand in the exact way that she did in my dream. Soon the light starts, and I have to look away from its blinding glare.

The light in front of my eyes dims so I no longer see the red of my eyelids, but now I see the fear on Kate's face. "How...how did he do it? I watched the death...but my view stayed on the body after you exited the room. It rebuilt itself and he stood again, as if he was alive. He could walk; stride even, without his cane. The headmaster is reanimated, alive."

"For a third time? That's interesting." I groan.

"Well, it looks like we have a job. We're going hunting." Tess says seriously.

Hunting, what an interesting term to use for what we're going to do. I didn't want to think of the possibility of my life ever becoming like a television show, it just seemed to strange and harsh. Hunting is supposed to be dear and game, not murderous people who kill others. Not any unnatural causes that walk the earth, this wasn't supposed to be a game.

Chapter 17

"That's ridiculous." I scream, and clutch my face in my hands. "How is that even possible??"

"How is that even possible?" Jaci repeats angrily.

"If you haven't realized, we're a sorcerer's family." Kate said. "He's a necromancer."

Well that made sense. The kids, strung up in the hall on the ceiling were obviously dead. It hadn't even crossed my mind that there was a very dark magic acting there. Necromancy was supposed to be the study of the line between life and death. It had become raising the dead to fight in eternal pain, causing agony to all that cross its path. How did I not notice that the headmaster was a sorcerer, and a powerful one at that? Resurrecting himself takes quite a bit of power, and a lot of knowledge of necromancy.

"Of course." Jaci says, bitter. "Let me guess, your mother was a witch?"

"No!" Kate huffs. "She was an arch mage, wielding the power of white magic."

Jaci pales. White mage married to a necromancer. It's uncommon, but it happens. It creates some very powerful magic....which must explain the very powerful child. "Where is your mother now?" I ask.

"She was slain by a necromancer in order to have her power sucked up, you must know what happens when light and dark magic collide." Kate says.

"Actually, I don't." Tess said.

"It's like magnets, opposites attract. The dark magic and the white magic, when combined, would have made that person the most powerful sorcerer in existence. They normally banned white mages and necromancers from even being friends, but for some reason my parents were exempt." Kate said. Kate went silent, then continued; "You don't think he....."

"He could have, he was incredibly powerful. It takes some serious juice to resurrect someone....especially twice. And so soon between goes." Jaci says.

"Did he ever speak of her?" Tess asks.

"No, he'd get mad when I mentioned her. Oh my goodness...is there a way I can find out if he killed her?" Kate asks, her voice is quiet.

"You're pretty powerful yourself. Take hold of his cane and look." I pitch in. If Kate finds out that her father killed her mother, she may just get the fuel she needs to join us in hunting him down and destroying him once and for all. Then we can go and live in peace.

Kate sits this time; I guess the glow thing is just for show. She closes her eyes and puts her hand on the cane, and for a long period of time she is as still as a statue. Tess, Jaci and I exchange glances while we wait for Kate to stand back up and tell us what's going on.

Half an hour passes and yet we haven't seen any change or movement in Kate. I guess digging through years of time takes...well...time. "I'm getting hungry." Tess complains.

"Well than eat." I snap.

"We don't keep food in the house because it's rare that we're here. More often than not we're on the road." Tess said. "Jaci, let's go. Will you drive me to like a taco bell or something so I can get us dinner?"

"I'll go instead." I snap.

"No, you can't both leave alone and we need someone here with Kate, but someone has to keep an eye on the driver." Tess complains.

"I don't want another girl to go off anywhere with my boyfriend, capuche?" I ask.

"You're too jealous. Come on, Jaci, let's go." Tess replies.

"Don't I get a say in this?" Jaci asks.

"No." Tess replies, and stalks out the door.

"Bratty little girl..." Jaci huffs as he follows her out into the darkening night.

"You're going to Taco Bell, right?" I call out the door after them, and all I get in return is the finger from Tess. Yowza. I just wanted a simple answer. I smirk to myself and close the door as the Dart pulls out of the drive way. "What am I going to do all alone with a statue-still sorcerer?"

I plop down on the couch, deciding on a nap. I close my eyes, tired, and soon I am fast asleep.

Wh....where am I? I open my eyes, not that it helps. It is completely dark in this room. There is absolutely no light anywhere, and the darkness is unsettling. I can feel it in the pit of my stomach, and it's an icy fist being punched through me. I turn, trying to open my eyes wider, trying to let in light, when slowly a glow starts rising from the space behind me.

It's slow, so slow. But the glow brightens into a burning light as I turn to face it. I shield my eyes, and try to peer into it. "I wouldn't suggest that." rings a clear, melodious voice. I close my eyes and feel the heat lifting off my face. The burning red I can see through my eyelids fades to a smooth black. "Go ahead and open them now." Says a familiar voice.

"Kate?" I ask as I open my eyes. "What are you, honestly?"

Her eyes are glowing blue fire, and her smirk is calculating. "I am something that you don't need to know, not yet. Now you asked what you were going to do with a statue-still sorcerer. You are going to talk to her, to plan with her. We're going on a journey."

"Where could you possibly take me like this?" I ask.

"Everywhere. I assume you've heard of astral projection?" Kate says calmly.

"Yes I have." I say, striding slowly towards her. "But, again, where are we going?" I ask.

"Into the past." Kate reaches out her hand. I take it and as our skin touches I feel a hot, searing pain. I cry out in agony, feeling my skin peel off my bone from the heat, and I feel as if I am melting. I close my eyes and grit my teeth against the pain and soon it becomes unbearable.

The pain stops. I wish I could say that some magical force stopped it or that it faded to tingles or even that I ended up dead. No. It just stopped, as if it hit a wall. I open my eyes questioningly, *wondering if I had actually died. I kicked myself for that thought, I wouldn't be thinking if I was dead. Would I?*

My eyes open to reveal a house. It's the exact house I was in before but it's alive, vibrant, and happy. The walls are deep blue with a cream trim, and there is a birthday party going on. I look around and see Kate standing next to a baby girl. The eyes are identical- is that Kate as a baby?

I stride over. "Kate, where are we? Or a better question would be; when are we?"

"This is my second birthday party. It was very hard to find this memory on the cane but I did it. I found it. This is the day my mom died." Kate says quietly.

"They can't hear us, right? No one can see us?" I ask, looking around as little children run dangerously close to me.

"Nope. We're alone." Kate says. Her voice sounds echo-y. That's a new feature.

"Let's trail your mom." I say.

Kate blushes. "I was going to say follow my dad, but you're right. If it was him, he'll be there. If not, we can find her real killer to track him down."

I smile brightly. "There we go. Now we just have to find your mom... do you know what she looks like?"

Kate pulls a small locket from under her shirt. In it is a picture of a beautiful woman with matching blue eyes. It must be a family gene or something. "This is who she is, we'll be able to find her. Just look for my eyes."

No, that wasn't creepy. I now had the thought of lone eyes rolling around on the floor, tangled in the optic wires, drowning in a pool of blood. Time to push THAT thought away! "We can't split up, we wouldn't be able to communicate so let's go." I reply.

We walk forward quietly, peering into the faces of long gone strangers, marveling as we watch old history unfold. "Kate, how old are you?" I ask her, wondering how long ago this party was.

"I'm your age, nearly 17." She replies. "My birthday is coming up soon."

"Ah." Enough with the small talk for now, we continue searching through eyes of old strangers. It isn't long before we stumble upon her mother.

Her mom is smiling brightly, the life and soul of the party. She is gentle and kind and her eyes hold warmth despite their icy color. There are laugh lines on her soft face and she is tall, and willowy in frame. Her hair, raven black, has a few gray strands intermingled with the black. It is long and in smooth waves. The wedding band on her finger has a dull sheen to it, as if lit by inner magic. Her smile is soft but genuinely happy. Why would anyone kill her for power?

Kate looks stricken as we mingle around her mother. "Honey, can I talk to you?" It is the headmaster, years younger. His hair is dusty brown, with gray streaks. He looks sour, as if he has drunken bad milk.

"Yeah, love, what's up?" Her mom's smile fades slightly as she looks at the headmaster. Her eyes flash up and stare at me, then at Kate, and her expression does not give into her confusion.

"Come with me, it's not a topic best discussed aloud." The headmaster says and turns, stalking away.

"I will talk to you two later." Her mom mutters to us, and then follows. We follow after her, and I am dumbfounded. How on earth did she see us? Is white magic all that powerful?

The headmaster leads them to what I would assume is their bedroom, and he closes the door behind her as she enters. My god I really hope they aren't about to do the nasty. Kate tenses up, gets very angry. "My mom was murdered in the bedroom."

"Oh, so it's NOT about to get really awkward?" I ask. Kate glares daggers at me and I smirk lightly, trying to get over the very serious, potentially awkward subject at hand.

"So, honey, you know how hard it is to have a necromancer as a husband. Try having the most powerful woman in the world as your wife. I think it should end. Us. I think you need to go." The headmaster said.

"You're asking for a divorce at your daughter's second birthday party?" Her mom asks angrily.

"No, no, not like that." The headmaster said. "Miranda, I'm asking you to give me your powers and you know the only way to do that; you have to die."

*"You're going to kill me. You think that you can overpower me? As you said yourself, **I am the most powerful woman in the world.** What do you think you can do about it?"*

"Little do you know, I've been drinking your blood bit by bit. As a necromancer, I learned that consumption of blood gives you a

small piece of their power. Without your knowledge, I've been taking your blood while you slept. Plus, by means of physical strength, I outrank you. This makes me the most powerful person in the world. And I want your power. Sorry honey," he spits out the word 'honey' like a rotten piece of meat, "but you have to die."

Kate clutches my arm, hard, as her dad stalks over to her mom. I see a smirk on her mother's face, her "nice-guy" demeanor is gone, and she takes a protective stance. A slight shimmer of white aura covers her, glowing slightly, as if it's body armor. She looks ready for a fight, and I suppose that is exactly what is going to happen.

I can't help but root for her, begging her to win, even though this is a time locked mystery. It's impossible to end any other way than for her to die, and Kate and I know it. It's hard to watch the battle, but it's incredible. Black magic seeps from the ground to swirl around the headmaster, cloaking him in darkness that puts the night to contest. From the cloak of black magic sprouts two twisted, dark daggers. Her mother stands with no weapon but the light swirling around her, and somehow I felt like she's much stronger at the moment, but realizes her fate.

She turns to face us. "So that's why you two are here..." She mutters.

"What did you say?" The headmaster snarls.

"It's funny how necromancers can only speak to those from the past. It's an honor to see my daughter, all grown up." Kate's mother turns and faces the headmaster once again. She closes her eyes and raises her hands, twitching her fingers as if typing on air.

The headmaster is confused and as the white magic fades from around his wife, he understands and cries "No!" and charges at her, daggers out stretched. The last wisp of the magic fades as the daggers pierce her heart.

"You will never know who got my white magic.... it's the girl with our daughter at this moment so many years later.... You will never have my power.... This is the moment she realizes it, when she sees my death...." Kate's mother gasps, and before long the light fades from her eyes.

Kate looks over at me, shocked and angry at the same time. Was her mother talking about me? The headmaster makes a dark figure, cloaks him, and makes him run from the room. The headmaster screams and following him, making the figure slightly faster. "Murder! Murder!!" The headmaster yells. I catch his slight smirk, yet apprehension in his eyes.

"It's time to wake up." Kate turns to me and says quietly. "I'll join your case, and he will die for what he did. I suppose your new-found white magic will come in handy."

"She said that I would know when it has been awakened in me. She said I would know as she died. I don't feel any different. I'm just a human, I guess, no white magic here." I say quietly.

"I'll bring Tess on the trip, maybe that's who she is talking about. Time stands still, but they're pulling into the driveway now and those tacos smell pretty good." Kate says.

Tacos! Kate places her hand over my forehead and my eyes close. When I open my eyes, headlights are shining through the windows as the car tires crunch up the driveway, and in moments Jaci and Tess walk in with two bags each.

"We have a lot to tell you." Kate says as she stands. I guess this is much better discussed with food, though."

Chapter 18

"So what you're telling me is," says Tess through a bite of taco, "You want me to travel back in time as a ghostly thing to see if I have a dead woman's white magic writhing inside me, waiting to be awakened?"

"Yeah, basically." Kate answers while munching on a burrito. Jaci and I are sitting close by each other, eating quietly.

Tess laughs. "Fine, yeah. After we finish eating though." She smirks and I feel angry. I wish it had been me, I could have saved Jaci and I from being hunted by the man who stole three years of our lives. It wasn't too fair, you know? "How do we know he won't win in the end?" she continues quietly.

"Because we won't let him." Kate replies strongly. "He murdered my mom, power hungry. He'll murder whoever has the white magic."

"I thought necromancers could take power by drinking blood?" Tess asks.

"Why would you know that? Plus, he would get the most of the power by killing the wielder. You wouldn't stand a chance, if you were ever on his side." I reply sourly.

Tess laughs. "You're just jealous that it isn't you."

"I am, but I'm not jealous of the fact that whoever has it will be hunted every day of their life once the power is awakened." I say bluntly. "If it's you, you're guaranteed to be murdered. You will never be able to have a lover that you can fully trust. You'll never be able to trust your children. You would never be able to trust anyone because they could be necro and they could turn on you. However, if a necro takes the power then there is nothing in the world that can stop them. Not one thing."

"Well I've lost my appetite." Tess said.

Kate nods and puts down her half eaten burrito. "I'm going to bring you, as an astral projection, into the period of time. If it awakens in you, we're going to need you to end this once and for all."

"Now?" Tess asks.

"Yes, now." Kate replies. "We really don't have time to spare before the mission."

"So now it's a mission?" Asks Jaci.

"Yes. I thought you wanted to kill him as much as I did!" Kate says.

"We all have our reasons, I guess. Tess doesn't, not yet. Hopefully she will soon." I answer.

"So I'm just a weapon, instead of a person sent to murder with a conscious?" Tess is sounding angrier and angrier.

"Hakuna your matatas, Chica." I reply to her. "We're getting rid of a serious murderer, someone who watched as children as young as 13 died by the hundreds, died in painful ways. He took a gun to the head of my best friend and her boyfriend when they tried to escape. He kidnapped Jaci and I in attempt to starve us so we would kill each other to survive. He's not even cruel, he's sadistic."

"He murdered my mother and lied to me for my entire life." Kate said quietly. "He may have even wronged you in some way, without you even realizing."

"He couldn't be responsible for-" Tess cuts off. "Come on, are we going to do this or not?!" Tess says angrily. I don't understand her sudden anger. She plops herself on the couch and instantly crashes. Kate shrugged at me, and sits in lily pose to start meditating once again.

I turn to Jaci. "What the hell just happened?" I ask.

"I don't know, but something is up. I really hope things go as planned, you know." He replies.

I know he's right. Something weird is definitely happening. I'm really tired though. I lean on Jaci's shoulder and soon enough I'm asleep.

"Well will you swear my life is safe, that you won't kill me for it. This is even if I get it, it could be someone else." I recognize that voice, it's Tess.

I try to look around for her, but everything is all black. I can't see anything. "I swear, we'll rule together as immortals. I would even take you as my wife, if you wanted. You certainly are pretty enough. The white magic, while inside you, would heal you of your illness forever." I know that deep, raspy voice.

"But Adam, what if I'm not the one with the power?" Tess asks.

"It would be no one else but you. I have been operating a school to cycle through all children who show any sign of promise of

the power, and have kept my daughter in seclusion. You must befriend her, gain her trust. And as soon as you get it, use it to come to me. I will be waiting, Tess. Now, answer me this." the headmaster says.

"Yes?" Asks Tess.

"Isn't it ironic? To have the world start for Adam and Eve, and have it fall below Adam and Tess Eve?"

"It is a bit odd. Why won't you tell me your last name?" Tess asked.

"True names are power." Adam answers.

I'm being shaken awake. "Whaaaat??" I ask, tiredly. I open my eyes to see Kate's wild, alarmed ones. "What is it?"

"Tess has the power but she bolted as soon as we got back. She's gone. I think she's a traitor." Kate cries.

"Yeah, she is." I reply. "I was honestly just dreaming about her with the headmaster. Is his name really Adam?"

"Yeah, you didn't know that? Anyway, we have to go find her! Stop her before she gets herself killed!" Kate shrieks.

"Curse her sudden but inevitable betrayal..." Jaci mutters, unnoticed. He looks around. "Oh, really? Did none of you get that? Firefly?" he sighs.

"She won't get very far, it's late and she's probably tired. Come on, let's go back to bed." I say.

"No! We have to go!" Kate says, panicking.

"It's dangerous and we are NOT strong enough without sleeping." Jaci inputs his opinion strongly.

Kate pauses, "...Fine! First thing in the morning, we are leaving."

"Did she take my Dart?!" Jaci calls, concerned.

"No. She...she ran. She ran out like a panther." Kate says, astounded.

"How on Earth are we going to deal with this? How old exactly is she? In my dream, Adam offered to marry her to guarantee her safety or something. As if he would keep that promise." I answer.

"That's gross." Jaci whispers.

Kate glares. "Power is like a flame, and people are like moths. They're bound to realize that she has the power, and she is in so much danger. We have to get to her first."

"But for now, we have to sleep." I continue. "I think we all agree."

Kate begrudgingly nods and Jaci asks "are there bedrooms we can use?"

"Separate?" Kate asks in return.

"No, preferably together." I reply to her.

"Good thing, because there are only two bedrooms." Kate replies. "Come on, they're upstairs."

On the way up the stairs we pass by a bathroom and I excuse myself to use it. When I'm back out, I'm alone in the hall and utterly lost. I really wish I had my Academy-issued backpack, I will only ever feel comfortable with it slung over my shoulder. I miss the familiar weight. I don't feel safe, although that isn't new, but I'm alone and unarmed. It's alarming, really. I jump about a foot in the air when Jaci pokes his head out of a bedroom and says my name. "A little warning would be nice." I giggle nervously, my heart pounding in my chest. I'm such a scaredy cat.

"Rae, it's not me." Jaci says from behind me.

I twist my head to look quickly, and see Jaci's silhouette on the other side. I back against the wall, and in the process hit the light switch. Light floods through the hallway and I see two of Jaci, and behind each of them a Kate. "What the heck is with my luck?" I mutter to myself.

Each Jaci stalks forward cautiously, and they're mirroring themselves-err, each other, perfectly. I am really torn, the copies are so exact that there is no difference in them. I'll have to base it on their personalities, I guess.

"Rae, this is really creepy. Believe me, it's the real me." Jaci 1 says.

"I have honestly never heard you call me Rae before." I answer.

"Back off of my woman." Snarls Jaci 2.

"Woah, neither of you are acting like my Jaci so would the shape shifter copy cat please stand up and tell me what it wants with me?" I ask in contempt.

Jaci 1 says "I want you because I love you."

"No you don't." Snaps Jaci 2. "You're working for someone to try to capture her."

The Kate's in the background are being quiet, that's very unlike them...her....whoever she is. I'm really confused and it's hurting my head. "Shape shifter, come back tomorrow and we'll play this game, right now I am as tired as anything and I just want to go to bed."

"Fine." Jaci 2 morphs into some weird, scaly creature and Kate 2 morphs into its tail. "I guess you don't want to hear about your quest, or where to find Tess."

"Tell us tomorrow, I am dog tired." I yawn.

"My god you are stubborn. Fine! Whatever! Goodnight Mrs. Freak show." The creature stalks and struts off.

My head starts hurting worse. "What on Earth has my life come to?" I ask.

Jaci walks out of the room and hugs me tightly. It's nice to smell his scent. It's comforting and soothes my headache right away. "Come on, off to bed." Jaci whispers to me.

I don't even remember crawling into bed or curling up to Jaci, but there I am. I'm nearly unconscious, and soon I fall asleep, but not before I cross my fingers and hope to dream.

Kate is kneeling, fist pressed to the floor and head bowed. "No, she does not know who or what I am yet."

"How is she supposed to trust you?! We are on her side. We are there to guard and protect her because you know of your mother's alterations. You've read the letter she wrote. Your mother was an impressive prophet and knew that she was going to die and nothing could have saved her. She had begun the transfer a very long time ago." A melodious female voice speaks.

"But, Selene, don't you think she'd be a bit confused? She could never believe it. Nor could her boyfriend. As a matter of fact he would take her and take off running. It is so new to have her on my side." Kate replies.

"Kate, you're an Archer. You know how to keep them safe, but in order to do that you must keep them close. Go after Tess, for I fear Adam will not keep up his end of the bargain. You know that if Tess dies, the transfer will begin and Reagan's life will always be hunted. Now, the sun draws near. You know Apollo is insulted when the moon stays for too long. Good morning, Kate, and goddess speed." Selene says to Kate, placing her hand gently on her head.

It takes so long for me to try to even understand what I just saw. Selene is just one of the many names for a lunar deity, or a goddess of the moon. I have no idea what an Archer is, although there is lore pertaining to Artemis's archers. Supposedly they will live forever unless they die in battle, and are unable to take the company of a man... It really makes a lot of sense about Kate, I suppose. It still doesn't explain why she has eyes of blue flame.

Chapter 19

We're packing anything useful that we can find, and believe me that is a lot. We find the packs that were given to us our freshman year, and the interior seemed bare without all my snagged knickknacks. It has the weapons and it has the BB's, the fireproof materials, and a flotation device.

We have to make a game plan, or else everything will fail miserably. I guess we're going to do it in the car. We're rushing around, yet actually finding everything we need to succeed. If the saying "dress for the job you want" actually applied in this situation, I would be a hunter hobo. It wasn't exactly high on my choice of occupation.

We gather not just weapons, but food and even camping supplies. I suppose you'll never know what life throws at you. "Jaci, will you go start up the car?" Kate calls.

"Yeah, start packing the trunk." He replies. I grab one of the bags (it is *heavy!)* and bring it outside. He pops the trunk and the early morning sunshine reflects off of it into my eyes. I walk into the shade cast by the open trunk and I put the bag in. I do this with all the bags, and Kate brings out the camping supplies. Jaci brings out our food and we close the trunk. There is hardly enough space in there.

I yell "Shotgun!" and climb, smirking, into the front seat. Kate rolls her eyes and stalks to the back seat, choosing the middle.

She pulls out a sleek iPod and AUX cord. "Plug it in; I've got a song I want you guys to hear."

I grab the smooth cord and plug it into the jack. Kate leans forward to allow the cord to reach, and taps her screen a few times. *"Today's a winding road, that's taking me to places that I didn't want to go....woah."*

"Hey, I know this song!" I cry out. "I love this song."

Kate beams happily. "So you've got good taste."

"Of course, look who she's dating." Jaci giggles.

I laugh, and for a moment life feels simple, normal. I feel like I'm on my way to the mall with friends, or something. Is this what normality feels like? I look out the window. If this is how it feels to be normal, I don't want any part of it. *"Your voice was the soundtrack of my summer; do you know you're unlike any other? You'll always be my thunder so bring on the rain, and bring on the thunder."*

Kate is humming this song in the back seat, and head banging. She's such a goof. I look out the windshield. "So... Does anyone know where to start?" I ask.

Kate leans forward and points. "Maybe we could start there. It seems pretty logical."

I lean forward and squint, and in the distance I can make out flames licking up toward the sky. I look closer, and notice that the flames are *blue*. Like sky blue with deep blue edges. "Yup, that seems like a safe assumption. Let's go that way."

Jaci glances at the flames and pulls into the right lane to turn off the highway. I grab the door handle as we go down the off ramp because it's a sharp turn. The road evens out and we find ourselves on a new, side road, lined by rows of wheat. It's such a shocking change from the trees I used to see whenever I was in the car with my parents. They just died a few days ago... I go quiet and continue looking out the window, over the waves of sheer golden wheat, waving in the breeze. I feel like there was an elephant in the car, all of the sudden. I've been with Kate for all of two days, and now we're off tracking down her friend-gone-rogue? Why do I feel like I'm being led directly to my death?

It takes a few minutes but soon we drive up to a portion of the road that's completely blocked off. There aren't cops blocking it off, but men in suits with earpieces. There are two standing in the road, and four in the two black cars blocking off the road. One of the men in black walks up saying, "Sorry, you can't go this way." When he gets to the car he says "You'll have t-oh hello there, you're allowed to go right in. We've been expecting you kids."

I glare at the man. "Wow. You are *sooo* original; I really hope your mommy is proud."

"At least my mother wasn't murdered at the hands of one of my coworkers." The man smirks. That stings.

These are some really poor "Yo Momma" jokes, so I decide to land the killing blow. "She will be."

Jaci looks at me. "Oh, and don't even think of backing up and leaving. You've delivered yourself directly to your death by our hands. Thank you very much for making my job much easier." The man smirks.

"So you kill kids for kicks. You are one sick fellow." I giggle. The giggle unnerves the man, and he walks away, waving us forward. Jaci, being sensible, goes with the flow. I think that it's both stupid and smart. I don't understand their threat about leaving, but we may actually be going to our death. If we have even a hint of a chance, though, this is it. It's incredibly stupid for Tess to base so damn near us, but again-she couldn't have gotten too far last night.

I'm wary as we park, and slowly get out of the car. Kate and Jaci follow slowly, unsure of what to do. "This way, kiddies!" Smirked the first man.

"Thank you, kind sir. Will you tell the valet I prefer a spot with shade? Also, we can bring in our own luggage, okay?" Jaci says. The first man grits his teeth; he's pissed at our strange cheeriness. I don't understand our false bravado, but it's truly all that we have. We are going up against something completely unknown, and we are going to try to kick its butt into oblivion. At least, I hope so. That's where the strange false bravado has come from, and I really hope it doesn't leave.

We quickly dash to the trunk and get our bags. "Whatever suits you best, kids, you're still going to lose, and you're still going to die. There's nothing you can do to stop them, so have your fun with it." The man grabs Jaci. "They said I could have you... they have no use for a mere mortal..." The man takes off his sunglasses as thick, coarse fur begins to push from his skin. His lower jaw cracks and juts forward, shaping his nose differently. His ears slide upward on his head as his skin slides down, thickening his neck. Loud, concerning snaps come from the man's spine as it grows longer, arching his back. The fur spreads down his arms like a wave, and Jaci winces as thick black claws extend from his fingertips, piercing his skin. "Do you want to watch this, Reagan?" The wolf-man says, voice guttural.

"Gimme a second, I want to record it." Kate says. I glare over at her and she shrugs. Confusion is evident on the wolf man's face. She reaches into her pocket and pulls out her iPod. "Hang on.... let me pull up the camera."

There is a tiny, almost undetectable light coming off of her fingertips. It could almost be mistaken for the iPod screen's light. Kate's fingers dance, not even touching the screen. The man can't see any of this, and he's too stunned and confused to question. "Alright, go ahead." says Kate. I reach for my scythe, but Jaci stops me. There is a mischievous look in his eyes. I'm pissed, but why am I left out of the loop?

Kate raises her iPod slightly and the silver shimmers, in what I'm assuming is the sunlight. The wolf man says "Now pay attention, Reagan! Watch as your boy toy dies!" He opens his jaw wide quickly, and dives in the bite Jaci's throat out. I run forward, scythe extended. From behind me flies a silver dart, striking the wolf man in the soft part of his inner throat. I whip around and see Kate, manipulating silver from her iPod, smirking there.

"You....how?' The wolf man rasps.

"Magic." Kate replies.

The other men who had been watching the ordeal now rushed at us, all transforming into wolves on the way over. "No." Growled the dying wolf man. "They'll meet with their fate inside. Just.... help me lay down now. Bring them inside. Don't let them leave without paying for this." Three of the men grab each of us tightly, shredding tendons in our arm with their thick claws. I cry out in pain and the dying wolf man smirks. What a bum.

Blood is flowing freely down my arm, but Jaci is in worse condition. His captor made a point to grab the arm that had been previously injured by the dying wolf man, in the exact location, in an attempt to cause him pain. By the grimace on Jaci's face, I could tell that it was working.

I wanted to break every bone in these wolves' bodies, and make them suffer for hurting him. I plan on it, once we get out of here alive; I'm going to wreck them. The men hurry us over to the doors which bang open noisily. "Look what the cat dragged in, murderous children." Snarls the bigger of the wolf men. "They killed one of us."

"Was it the alpha, the one I had promised Jaci to?" A cool voice sends chills of anger down my spine. Tess walks forward, revealing herself and the source of the voice.

"Yes ma'am." Answers the wolf man.

"Good. I wanted him dead, he's bad in bed." Tess says.

"What on earth are you wearing? Guuurrrllll, why do your shoes match your outfit?" I say, trying to lift even a portion of my anger. Anger is pointless and senseless and will get me killed.

Tess's outfit, I have to admit, is really freaking sweet. She's wearing a white robe that looks like it's made for her and her power. It's form fitting, hugging her shape and it's so long that it pools around her feet. The low stoop neck barely hugs her shoulders before clinging tightly to her arms. The sleeves were long and formed a sort of glove covering the back of her hands.

There are black lines, about an inch thick, extenuating down the sides of her robes making her look sickly thin. Thick black makeup surrounds her eyes and her hair, a natural blonde, shines gold with an inner light. In her hand is a twisted oak staff, which seems to be humming with life. On her finger is a big, fat ring. "Hello, my friends."

"You don't have friends." Kate calls. "You're nothing to anyone."

There is hurt in Tess's eyes, but she soon crushes it and replaces it with cool detachment. "Would you all like to formally meet my fiancé, the reason we're all gathered here today?"

"You know Tess, you are nasty." Jaci says.

Tess glares at him. "At least I'm marrying someone I love."

"The man who murdered the only woman he ever truly loved in order to try to get her power. You know he was going to bring her back, but he couldn't. He wasn't strong enough." Kate says. It must be hard for her to talk about this, as it was her father-the man who murdered her mother. Talk about a dysfunctional family.

Jaci says quietly "I'm going to marry her one day." He glances over at me.

Hold the phone; when did my life switch to romance from gruesome, sci-fi fantasy? I crave, more than anything, to be as normal as everyone else. It just isn't in my favor, the cards don't fold correctly. I obviously want to marry him but I know we'll either die or be hunted for forever. We have no choice but to live this life, as fugitives.

"I'm tired of playing games. It's time for you to meet the man who runs the show, the real mastermind. Adam, will you come meet our guests?" Tess calls.

Of everything, of all the nasty shocks in the world, I never expect what I see next. Adam walks out from wherever he was hiding, and there is no cane with him. He walks with a straight back, and even looks a good 20 years younger. His face is fresh. When he speaks, there is no rasp in his voice. "Hello children, we've been expecting you." Considering what Tess is wearing, it's incredibly strange to see Adam in jeans and a batman tee shirt.

Kate recoils in horror. "You...have the audacity to wear that? The very outfit that you slaughtered my mother in?"

"Of course. It's become a tradition to slay lovers in this outfit." Adam says. Before Tess can react, he whips around. The blade of shadows that so long ago killed Kate's mother is seen, no light penetrating the darkness. He quickly stabs it straight into her gut, and pulls it in an upward motion, tearing her apart. Her intestines and organs tumble out, staining her clothing so dark red that it's nearly black. "Almost lovers, anyway. She had always thought it would be the cancer to kill her. It was always me killing her."

Tess's white magic attempts to fix her ruined body, but the wounds are too great. Great gasps of pain and surprise come from Tess, as she falls dying to the floor. Her gaze trains on me, her eyes soaking with ruptured blood veins. She dies in agony, and the expression remains frozen on her face. There is to be no peace for her.

Adam, once again the evil headmaster, stands laughing. He takes the ring off Tess's finger and tossed it to Kate. "Here, have a family heirloom. It was your mother's engagement ring."

"You monster." Kate whispers brokenly.

"Isn't that the point? Now the white magic is mine, and I can kill you pathetic excuses of mortals. Then I can move on with my life and do what I do best-kill." Adam says.

"So, were you born in November? I heard most serial killers were." Jaci says.

"You know, Jaci, you really need to be punished." Adam sighs. "If I hadn't killed your parents I'm sure they could do it for me. But they'd be too lenient. Watch me for a bit, and then I'll give you your punishment, mmmkay?"

Adam, while watching us, places his hand on Tess's shredding stomach, ignoring the squelch of intestines. White wisps of energy swirl around his hand, and like lint in a vacuum it's sucked into his hand, absorbed. He stands, and the white magic follows his hand like a jagged cloud. It is all absorbed, leaving Tess a shriveled, pure white corpse with deep black wrinkles. She becomes mummified, as every essence of even a soul is stolen.

The headmaster starts laughing. His laugh is a deep, throaty laugh that unsettles my very soul. Lightning crackles around him, striking the ground and shaking us off our feet. "Are you ready Jaci? Are you ready for your punishment?"

Jaci just glares hard at the headmaster. The headmaster shrugs. With a twist of his fingers I hear a thunderously loud *crack* and a thud. Jaci shouts hoarsely and late screams. I can't feel anything, and I can't move. "You monster!" Screams Jaci, his voice breaking. "You killed her! How did you get past our bracelet's power??"

"I am a god, child. I have all this power, I am invincible! Not only that, the Academy is no longer mine. I am not affiliated; therefore I pass the power of the bracelet." He replied.

I feel mental dread, but I can't feel it in the pit of my stomach. Where is my stomach? Why is my mind so empty, nothing more than thoughts? I stand and walk up to the headmaster, but I can't sense anything. I'm confused and scared. Where is the part of my mind that lets me control my body? I'm up close now. "I'll let you see her. She's here. She gets to watch you suffer." The headmaster says, and reaches forward to touch my forehead. I gasp, and no air comes. I turn, with no control, and see Jaci holding a lifeless body and sobbing, Kate kneeling next to him. Those are my converse, what are they doing on that body?

Jaci looks up, tear tracks on his face. "You killed her."

M-me. Me. I'm dead. But I'm here? But I'm in Jaci's arms. That's me. My favorite boot cut jeans, faded superman sweater that's too small in the arms. My messy curls. My face, broken, my neck jerky and twisted. I can't feel the nausea that I'm sure is building up, the fear. "I am the strongest man in the world, and I've just killed my only opponent. Reagan, you're dead. You can't talk, you're under my control. How do you feel?"

I open my mouth, "h-o. Ho-w?"

"How did you do that, you're dead! The dead don't talk. Ever." The headmaster says.

I turn my head, and it's unnerving to see my own body not respond. Jaci's normally brown hair is slowly streaking black, but it's hardly noticeable. I notice it.

Jaci slowly untwists my destroyed neck and looks up with pure fury, "I am going to kill you and bring her back." He stands up slowly. "You are going to die."

The headmaster just laughs. "You're going to kill the most powerful man in existence? HA. Good luck."

"I don't need luck." Jaci replies. "You're dead."

Chapter 20

"You're really going to regret everything." Jaci says, standing. His face is dark with rage, and his hair is slowly getting darker. "Either you bring her back or I am going to. Either way you're going to die, slowly and painfully. Just the way you deserve."

"You think you could possibly kill me?" The headmaster laughs, believing himself to be funny. "You don't know what power is. You are nothing, nothing more than an angry mortal who believes he can take me on."

"I'm going to help him." Kate said. "You killed my mother. You killed my friends. You killed innumerable kids. You really have to pay."

The headmaster pales slightly when Kate speaks, but quickly regains his cool and snaps "You really are an awful daughter, aren't you? An awful pixie, too."

"I'm the best and you know it." Kate snarls.

"If you're the best they have to offer, well, why haven't they died out yet?" The head master chuckles.

"D-d..Di..." I tremble, forcing the words from my mouth. Not the one that's dead on the floor, I doubt it could move.

"Shut up darling. No one really cares. Dead don't talk." The headmaster says slowly.

"Why are you such a jerk?" Asks Kate. "You really never deserved to be born."

"You would never have been born." The headmaster warns.

"I don't really care. Just, before we kill you, tell us why you did it. Why did you kill my mom? Why did you open the Academy? Why did you hunt these students?" Kate said.

"Do you really want story time before you're put permanently to sleep?" The headmaster sighs. "Fine. Listen close because I'm only going to say this once." I turn very slowly to face him. "Will you STOP THAT?" He yells at me. "That's really uncanny and kind of freaky. Anyway, if you want to know why, listen.

"I had to find it, the lost power. I had only intended to kill Anna, and that was only after I found out it was impossible to take her power without her death. I loved her, I truly loved her. It haunted me for years until I had frozen myself enough to do it. I killed her and her power fled. Instead of defending herself from me, she put a kink in her magic to send it off to Tess. Now Tess is dead and I don't understand the letter Anna left me... 'The dead will live.' That is the only thing she said. She must have known I was coming for her. I don't really understand what it has to do with her power though..."

"Will you carry on? There's supposed to a bid, deadly battle soon, we're supposed to slaughter each other, hello? Why did you start the Academy?" Jaci snaps.

"Touchy little boy. I started the Academy to find the one with the power. I hadn't known it was Tess, you know, not until Kate brought her home for the first time. Her only friend you know, a fake one. I spoke to her then, promised her safety, promised her love. That was when I implanted a disease in her, gave her cancer, so she would suffer. If she had died, the power would have lay hidden until a new successor rose. I would have hidden it. Don't you understand, the mixing of light and dark magic lends immortality to the wielder? I will never age. I will never die. This is why you will lose. I cannot lose! The only one who ever had a chance at beating me is dead on the floor beside you and only I can bring her back!"

That makes things harder. I feel so weighted down, heavier than I did while alive, like more than gravity was pulling me down. I didn't know why I was being pulled down, I wasn't exactly the worst person in the world. Was I? In my defense, every person I'd murdered wasn't a person, but a monster hell-bent on killing me for fun. Seriously, my struggles. It could be all the necromancy in the room, swirling around me, ready to pull my soul into whatever deed they need. I don't like that. "Bac-k." I stammer. Talking is really hard.

Why am I still trapped here? Am I just doomed to watch my only two friends in the world die? I want to be back in my body, to help them. I don't fully understand what Kate is. What exactly is a pixie? Jaci, unfortunately, is just human. There is no way that I can ever be returned-I am an archangel's blade in the hand of the devil and it's impossible to win me back.

"Now, can we carry on with me killing you or do you want to chat a bit more?" The headmaster eyes Jaci suspiciously. "Jaci, did you dye your hair?"

"Not recently, why does that even matter?" Jaci replies.

"It's darker than I remember." The headmaster comments. "No matter, the color of your hair won't last. Your hair itself won't last; it's going to wither away in your hole. No coffin for you, no marker, no gravestone. Just death."

"You sure do love happy endings, huh?" Asks Jaci.

"Only when they're for me!" Cackles the headmaster.

"Are we seriously doing this? Standing around and talking like children? Or are we going to get this show on the road and kill one another already?" Kate asks stubbornly.

"So eager to die, my daughter?" The headmaster asks. "So be it... unless you want to come home to my side. Last chance to live."

"And die the way my mother did? The way Tess did?' Kate asks. "I'd rather go down fighting you; hopefully I can drag you with me."

"So be it." Sighs the headmaster. "I just wish you would understand."

"What on earth could ever justify murder?" Jaci asks angrily. "Mass murder at that?"

"I've told you! I never wanted it to come to this! It was Anna's fault, Kate's mother's fault! Had she just let me take the power, many people would still be alive!" Adam yelled.

"What would you have done with that power anyway?" Screams Kate.

"Research. I would have been a god! I want to know what happens with the two powers mix and now look at me! I've won it, and you know it. Now die in pieces." Adam says.

Jaci falls to his knees and picks up my body, placing his hand on my forehead. The swirling pull around me got tighter, taking away any breath that I would have and crushing my spirit in a vise. I squeeze my eyes closed in discomfort and shriek.

It's a loud, resounding shriek that reverberates off the walls, vibrating my vocal cords. I'm hurting all over, in pain that feels like my bones are melting. My eyes fly open and I shriek again, looking up and the ceiling. There is something warm around me- scratch that, two warm things around me. Dizzy, I turn my head to face Jaci. I'm lying in his arms. "I thought I was dead." I whisper. "Am I?"

"Not anymore." Jaci says, and helps me to his feet. His eyes are very dark, and his hair is midnight black. That's a new look on him.

I stand woozily, and face the headmaster. "Hug it out?" I smirk.

"How is that, in any way possible? Jaci has no read, no physical prowess that would suggest necromancy. You're basically mortal, but invisible necromancer? That's new." The headmaster says quietly. "I'll just have to kill her again."

"Dude, give me a hug first." I say.

"Why the heck do you want a hug?" Adam asks.

"I was hanging out with your wife, she asked me to hug you for her." I reply.

"I don't do hugs." Adam says.

"A handshake, then. For Anna, your wife." I say and extend my hand. "I'm just a mortal, I'm without any power. No weapons look." I drop my back pack and walk forward slightly with my hand still extended.

"This isn't a peace treaty," huffs the headmaster. "This is a show of faith for my wife." He extends his hand to meet mine, and we shake.

It's an awkwardly long shake, but mostly because our hands seem to be suction cupped together. We yank hard, trying to pull apart our hands. The headmaster pulls out a large knife and swings, and just before I lose my hand we stumble apart. We're falling backward to the floor as his knife swings through blue, white, and black mist between our hands.

"No!" Yelled the headmaster. "That's mine! Give it back to me!"

Woah. The mist felt like it was flowing through my bloodstream, bringing peace and chaos to my nerves, setting me on fire with the coolest ice. I felt like I was literally glowing with power, like I could destroy the world with creation. The mix of the light and the dark was perfectly stable and balanced, and when the mist finally stopped coming I felt giddy enough to run into the stars.

"Woah...." I say, repeating my thoughts. I look at the headmaster and I could see everything. He was old, the draining of the power aged him greatly. His skin was sagging while clinging to his bones. His hair was slowly falling out, strand by strand. I could see his soul, black with golden edges. He was mortal again, but evil.

I look at Jaci and Kate, and they gasp at me. I see the purple and light blue that seems to cling to Kate, and tiny iridescent wings that couldn't be seen before. Pixie it is. Jaci has a deep green aura that is now tinged with black, lively but necro. I turn back to the headmaster and focus, holding out my hand. I squeeze my hand into a tight fist and smooth ice juts from either hand; forming a long, smooth staff in my hand. The top curls into jagged points, with a smooth part between thorns of ice. I grab the top of the staff by the smooth part and smash the handle, and pull a sharp sword from the wreckage. "I've always preferred warriors to mages." I say smoothly.

I swing my sword at lightning speeds and tap it to the collarbone of the headmaster, pressing down hard so he sinks to his knees. "M-mercy!" stammers the head master dryly. "Please!"

"Where was your mercy for all the children you murdered, for the creatures you sent to their death, and to Anna?" My voice was full of authority and pride, clearer and lighter than normal. I sounded like a bell. "Kate, do I have your permission?"

"Reagan, you're an Archangel. My permission means nothing." Kate replies.

"Your permission means everything." I reply. "I will do it unless you say no. He is your kin, after all."

"Do what you feel is right. Bring him to justice." Kate says. I can hear the pain but firm resolve in her voice. This man hurt her with betrayal, lies, and murdered her mother. She would miss him but she knows it has to be done.

"Kate..." The headmaster says weakly. He looks down at the floor, nothing more than human, and then nothing at all.

I turn back to Kate and Jaci, the head of the headmaster rolling around behind me, and run my hand next to the blade of my sword turning it into a staff once again. "Now, why do you two look like you've seen a ghost?"

"Not a ghost. Reagan, he killed you because you were the only one who could have stopped him. You heard my comment, you're an archangel. You have *wings.*" Kate said.

"So do you girly." I reply.

"I do?!" Kate gasps happily. "That mean's I've made a right choice. A big one, too."

"So, uh, Reagan. Have you noticed that your eyes are gold?" Jaci asked.

"No, but I really haven't had time to look in a mirror." I smirk.

"What do we do now? Do we part and go our separate ways?" Kate asks.

"I'm not leaving Reagan's side." Jaci says firmly.

"What if you do the same thing my dad did? Reagan, I wouldn't trust him in the slightest. You'll be unable to trust anyone ever again because for the rest of eternity someone will want your power. It is literally a gift and a curse." Kate warns.

"Jaci is soul bound to me. He raised me from the dead, linking his power with mine. The instant he tries to harm me or my soul, or even my power, he will drop dead because the soul connection will break." I say. I roll back my shoulders and feel great wings expand. I look to my left; my wings are easily 6 feet long on each side. They are black with white tips and streaks. I roll my shoulders some more and feel the delicate contract of light bones, and when I look over my shoulder they're not there.

"Those are some fabulous accessories." Jaci says in awe.

"They really are." I giggle. For the first time in years, I'm at peace. The man who took my life and flipped it upside down is dead forever. I'm some sort of mythical being. I must have had it in me for a long time, my whole life, but as an empty shell that burst into life when my power was awakened.

"Things have changed for me, and that's okay." Jaci says.

I glare at him. "Did you just..."

"Quote song lyrics? Yes. Yes I did." Jaci says.

"The end of our issues is here, guys, so I think we can afford something to eat." Kate said. "I am starving."

"This is our last meal together though." Jaci warns. "Alright? Feel free to call us up but I've got to protect Reagan. Betrayal can come at any time."

"Fine, I understand completely." Kate replies.

"So... Let's go." I say.

We walk outside, seemingly unharmed. The remaining wolves were stalking around Jaci's car, remarking if they like it or not. When they hear the doors close they don't even look up. "Boss, can we eat them?" Says the shortest one.

"Yeah, have fun." I call.

In shock, the wolves all look up at us. "How did you survive?" Yelps the biggest one.

I unfold my wings and the wolves flinch, scared. I tweak my fingers and they drop, dead from broken necks.

I hide my wings again and Jaci and Kate just kind of glance at me. I chuckle to myself; it's really nice to have this power. I'm not going to be anyone like Adam was, although I have the blood of 4 men on my hand since I gained the power.

I was determined to help someone. As I climbed into the passenger seat the sun glinted into my eyes, and I smile lightly. It kind of seemed like a promise, a new day. Jaci brought us to In-and-Out burger, delicious. We were eating and talking and just enjoying our last few moments together.

"Where do you want me to drop you off?" Jaci said. "Is there a certain place you want to go?"

"No, I'll be fine on my own. This is the last time you will see me, too. I don't plan on ever seeing you two again, because it's on my head." Kate replied. "What will you do? Your entire life, you will be hunted. You will never have any peace, you will never no rest, or comfort."

"I think we will." I say quietly. "But don't worry about us; we'll be just fine."